## ABOUT THIS BOOK

**From *USA Today* bestselling author J.L. Weil comes the sequel to *Falling Deep*, where the truth can be a dangerous game.**

Mallory Dorian only wanted a normal, boring life. To graduate high school, go off to college—basically, do everything the opposite of her mom. But life has a way of interfering with her carefully laid out plans.

Insert Torent Stark, the drool-worthy demon who makes her want to throw away all her dreams. But before Mallory can open her heart, a dark shadow of death looms inside.

Mallory must face the past before she can think about the future, and her family's history has a few dark spots. It is up to her to break the blood curse looming over her family or risk all that she has grown to love.

# HAVENWOOD FALLS HIGH BOOKS

*Written in the Stars* by Kallie Ross

*Reawakened* by Morgan Wylie

*The Fall* by Kristen Yard

*Somewhere Within* by Amy Hale

*Awaken the Soul* by Michele G. Miller

*Bound by Shadows* by Cameo Renae

*Fata Morgana* by E.J. Fechenda

*Forever Emeline* by Katie M. John

*Reclamation* by AnnaLisa Grant

*Avenoir* by Daniele Lanzarotta

*Avenge the Heart* by Michele G. Miller

*Curse the Night* by R.K. Ryals

*Blood & Iron* by Amy Hale

*Shadows & Spells* by Cameo Renae

*Falling Deep* by J.L. Weil

*Saving Infiniti* by Rose Garcia

*Willful* by Liz Ferry

*Cast in Moonlight* by Ali Winters

*Promise the Moon* by Kallie Ross

*Blurred Lines* by Daniele Lanzarotta

*Ascending Darkness* by J.L. Weil

*Finding Infiniti* by Rose Garcia

*Unicorn's Lament* by Megan Linski

*Paper Bird* by Amy Richie

*Predestined* by Valia Lind

*Rediscovered* by Morgan Wylie

*Ashes of Fate* by Apryl Baker

Stay up to date at <u>www.HavenwoodFalls.com</u>

# ALSO BY J.L. WEIL

**DRAGON DESCENDENT SERIES**

*Stealing Tranquility*

*Absorbing Poison*

*Taming Fire*

*Thawing Frost*

**THE DIVISA SERIES**

*Losing Emma: A Divisa novella*

*Saving Angel*

*Hunting Angel*

*Breaking Emma: A Divisa novella*

*Chasing Angel*

*Loving Angel*

*Redeeming Angel*

**LUMINESCENCE TRILOGY**

*Luminescence*

*Amethyst Tears*

*Moondust*

*Darkmist – A Luminescence novella*

**RAVEN SERIES**

*White Raven*

*Black Crow*

*Soul Symmetry*

**BEAUTY NEVER DIES CHRONICLES**

*Slumber*

*Entangled*

*Forsaken*

**NINE TAILS SERIES**

*First Shift*

*Storm Shift*

*Flame Shift*

*Time Shift*

**HAVENWOOD FALLS HIGH SERIES**

*Falling Deep*

*Ascending Darkness*

**SINGLE NOVELS**

*Starbound*

*Casting Dreams*

*Ancient Tides*

# ASCENDING DARKNESS

## A HAVENWOOD FALLS HIGH NOVELLA

### J.L. WEIL

*For all those who encouraged and supported my dreams.*

# CHAPTER 1

The window in my bedroom was closed and yet, for an instant, I smelled the sea, heard the call of the water, felt its coolness wash over my face. Here and then gone. The longing to be in the water swelled in my heart, like an endless love.

Not that I knew a lot about love.

Why Torent Stark's face instantly flashed in my head at the mention of love was something I'd rather not dwell on. In fact, I'd rather not think of him at all. Too bad my mind didn't feel the same way.

Torent was a boy.

Okay, he wasn't just any boy. First, he was a half-demon. That right there was a giant red flag waving in my face and should have been enough to tell me he was bad news. Then there was the crazy ex-girlfriend drama. Torent's ex-girlfriend had made me her archenemy. Sometimes too much baggage was not worth the risk, but my heart didn't seem to care about his past relationships or the dark streak inside him he worked so hard to hide and control. I gave him mad props. He had so much more control over his abilities than I did.

My magnetic energy was still unstable, causing inconvenient

outbursts, like the time a box of staples almost embedded itself into one of my instructors at Sun and Moon Academy during one of my night classes.

What I was going to do about Torent was another one of those mysteries of life, and damn if my life hadn't become a long Nancy Drew novel. So much secrecy shrouded my past, and I was only recently unearthing the answers, but I had more questions.

Before moving to Havenwood Falls, my life was normal. I'd lived in Wisconsin, gone to an average high school, watched my mother end yet another marriage. And in a way, things had returned to that habitual norm. Mom got a job, which Gigi was thrilled about. I had settled in at school and was coming to terms with being a water nymph.

Okay, so not your typical normal, but my life was average by Havenwood Falls standards.

However, some things never change.

Take Brooklyn Kendall, for instance. She still hated my guts. Turns out she didn't need a magical object to feel such strong enmity for me.

Torent was still trying to get me to go out with him. He was persistent—I'd give him that. And cute. And charming. And . . .

A bird squawked outside my window, interrupting my internal list of all of Torent's redeeming qualities. At this time of the year, the local birds had already migrated south, but a few stragglers had taken up residence in the tree outside my window. They had spent the last week waking me up before my alarm, and that put them on my shit list. I was not a morning person, not before at least two cups of coffee. I hadn't thought much about it, but this morning, something about the sound gave me the heebie-jeebies.

My eyes narrowed, and I went to the window to push aside the curtain and peer out into the yard. The sun was just peeking over the mountains and, it being late November, the air would be brisk. A light sheet of snow carpeted the grass.

Perched on an icy branch, the black bird gave another warning screech. His midnight feathers were in stark contrast against the barren tree. Beady eyes of charcoal watched cautiously through the glass. Strange. His feathers ruffled as he stretched out his wings, and I smiled, tapping lightly on the window.

"Where are all your little friends?" I asked, not really thinking about the fact I was talking to a bird.

He cocked his head to the left and right, eyeing me. Then he kicked off the little branch and flew straight into the window. *Thwack.* I jumped back, unable to believe what had happened.

The bird had just committed suicide.

A blotch of blood smeared down the glass, and my stomach turned. I backed away, feeling uneasy about what I'd seen. It wasn't every day I witnessed a bird snapping its own neck.

So much for that *normal* life.

My cell phone buzzed on the bed, and I turned my back to the massacre streaming down my window to pick up my phone.

"Crap," I grumbled, staring at the time on my phone. My third alarm had gone off, and if I didn't move my ass, I would be late for school.

I tossed on a pair of jeans, a white tank top, and a flannel, only to stop in front of the mirror. *Dear God, is that me?*

My hair looked like one of those black birds had made a nest in it, blond curls messily framing my face. The mascara I was too lazy to remove last night was smeared over my eyes, giving me a Goth look. I was going to have to roll with it. On my way out the door, I snatched a tube of lip gloss and applied it hastily to my lips, then sprayed two squirts of perfume over my clothes, unsure if they were clean or not. I grabbed a brush, my car keys, and my book bag before dashing down the stairs into the kitchen.

Gigi was sipping a mug of hot coffee.

"Morning." She grinned cheerily.

I grumbled an inaudible response and plucked her cup of coffee from her hands, downing half of it. "Thanks. I needed that."

"I guess so," she replied, taking back the nearly empty cup. Her blue eyes were shining. For a woman in her sixties, Gigi was sharp as a whip.

Mom came around the corner and stopped halfway to the coffeepot, eyeing me. "What happened to your hair?"

She was dressed in black slacks and a white button-down shirt, one button too many undone at the top. No one was more shocked Mom had gotten a job as a file clerk at Bishop Enterprises than Gigi.

The two of them constantly harped at one another. It was as routine as taking the garbage to the curb on Wednesdays.

"Don't ask," I mumbled, moving through the kitchen. I threw a hand in the air, waving bye, and stepped out the front door.

Icy breezes wrapped around me, and a blast of wind blew through my flannel. I cursed myself for not grabbing a to-go mug of coffee. It would be a long-ass day. Not to mention what this wind was doing to my already disastrous hair.

Jogging down the stone path to my old and semi-reliable car, I twisted my head toward the tree outside my bedroom window, my thoughts returning to the bird. I didn't have to time check on his little corpse, and yet I found myself moving off the path and onto the lawn. The frozen grass crunched under my weight. I grew closer, and eventually my Converses skidded as my steps faltered.

*What the—*

There wasn't just one poor dead bird under the aspen tree. There were at least half a dozen strewn over the cold ground, their small necks angled oddly off to the side. My heart knocked in my chest.

My hand flew to my mouth, and I took a step backward. A trickle of unease ribboned down my spine as I tried but failed to make sense of the scene in front of me. What had happened here? I wanted to believe it was a natural event, not something supernatural, but I couldn't shake the sneaky suspicion it wasn't Mother Nature at play.

God, it would be just like Brooklyn Kendall to arrange a bird graveyard to freak me out. Things between my fellow water nymph and me were anything but smooth sailing. She still wanted to make my life miserable and blamed me for pretty much everything wrong in her seemingly perfect life. Misery loves company, as the saying went.

I suppressed a shiver and got into my car, backing out of the driveway with enough speed to kick up gravel.

I whipped my car into the parking lot of Havenwood Falls High. The three-story red brick building was bustling with students rushing to get to class. Throwing my car into park, I sat staring at the arched front doors and considered skipping the entire day. The whole dead-bird thing had gotten to me, more than I realized.

But ditching classes would earn me a Saturday detention and would tarnish my pristine college resume. I had a plan. That plan didn't involve me being stuck in Havenwood Falls for the rest of my life.

A world existed behind these mountains and waterfalls, and I was going to see it all. I *was* going to get that college scholarship. No deranged pranks or cute boys were going to stop me from pursuing my dreams.

I dashed through the front doors as the bell for first period rang. Son of a bitch. I was late. Again. My feet flew over the brown marble floor toward my first class. No time to stop at my locker.

"I hope this isn't going to become a weekly occurrence, Ms. Dorian," Mr. Zander, my AP English Lit teacher, scolded while I was sneaking not so stealthily into class.

I slumped into my seat, a tight smile pasted on my lips. "I wouldn't dream of it."

He went back to waving the black marker in the air, telling the class to open their textbooks to page seventy-three.

What a way to start the day.

I managed to get through my morning classes. Silver and blue snowflake decorations lined the cream hallways for the upcoming holidays. There always seemed to be some school event going on. HFH's mascot was a dragon. How fitting. The fierce-looking dragon was plastered everywhere—floors, walls, banners, flyers—you name it and he was there.

I slid my butt into the seat across from Beck, who was picking at something under his nails. Someone had given his hair color a boost last night. The blue was extra bright today.

"You know I'd dye your hair for you," I said, grabbing one of his hands and surveying the damage to his fingers. The skin was tinged blue, along with the tips of his nails.

He pulled his hand back to his side of the cafeteria table. "It looks so damn easy in the commercials."

I rolled my eyes. "You're supposed to wear gloves."

His nose wrinkled in disdain. "They make my hands sweat."

My brows rose in question. What was the big deal with a little hand sweat? It beat having blue fingers for a week.

"Wolf thing," he stated. "I was thinking of painting my nails black anyway."

Beck Winslow was the first real friend I'd made in Havenwood Falls. He was also a wolf shifter. Not a big deal in a town full of supernaturals.

I pushed aside some of my wayward second-day hair. "You're not going to believe the morning I've had."

"Hello, blue fingers," he replied, waving his hand in the air. "There is definitely something funky in the atmosphere. I'd say we're in for a snowstorm. I can smell it." His eyes shifted to the large square window that overlooked the parking lot.

That wasn't quite what I had in mind, and despite the sun beaming this morning, an incoming storm would explain the hint of water I sensed in the air. My eyes followed his, seeing the beginnings of gray clouds rolling in. "Is weather predicting a wolf thing?"

He grinned, and it lit up his face. "Intense senses."

My fingers drummed on the tabletop beside my untouched salad. What had possessed me to get rabbit food when what I really wanted was an entire pizza from Napoli's?

"I might need to borrow your intense senses," I said, half joking.

Beck plucked a cherry tomato from the top of my lunch and popped it into his mouth as he leaned over the table. "What's up?"

I nibbled on my lower lip instead of my salad. "This morning, a bird flew into my bedroom window, but that wasn't the strangest part. When I left for school, there were half a dozen dead birds scattered outside my bedroom. Tell me that is normal?"

"*That* is a bad omen, chica."

"Peachy," I said dryly. "Just what I need. So you're saying I should be worried?"

He shrugged. "It's hard to say. This time of year the animals get a little restless. It could be nothing. Oooor," he dragged out, "you might be cursed. Piss someone off lately?"

I sighed and leaned my head into my hands. "That narrows it down."

His eyes spanned the lunchroom, landing on a trio of girls giggling annoyingly. "I can think of one particular popular girl who would love to throw a flock of dead birds at your house."

In sauntered the bitch of the hour.

Brooklyn Kendall.

Would she really do that? Yes, although it didn't explain the bird flying into my window. But the other birds dead on the ground? I wasn't sure. The whole thing smacked of some devious plot Brooklyn would concoct.

The devil herself was giving me a mad case of the stink eye as she crossed the cafeteria with Leena and Cora in tow.

"Is this feud between us ever going to end?" I muttered.

Beck's sparkling gray eyes trailed the nymph squad. "I hope not."

I playfully smacked him on the arm. "Dude, that's not funny."

He rubbed at the spot on his bicep, grinning. "I can't help it. Things have been so much more . . . colorful since you moved in."

My head tilted to the side while I regarded him. "What's the name of your therapist again? I think it might be time to switch your meds."

He laughed, throwing back his blue head and gaining the

attention of a few tables surrounding us. "See, this is what I'm talking about. This school needed you, Mal."

I wasn't so sure about that. Brooklyn blamed me for ruining her life. Her ex-boyfriend was derailing me from my life plan. Mom put on a brave face, but I could tell something had her worried. And I had unruly magnetic powers. None of these were things I construed as good.

# CHAPTER 2

*S*torms never really bothered me. Maybe it was my connection to water that offered calm during the howling of the winds, the crash of thunder, and the spears of lightning slashing across the black sky. Beck had been right. Havenwood Falls was in for a helluva storm, and for the end of November, ice was definitely in the forecast. For now, the sky was putting on quite the show.

I raced across the parking lot to my car, my bag jostling behind me. The last place I wanted to be caught was on the road when the mixture of rain and ice decided to fall. My steps faltered at the sight of Torent leaning against my Chevy Malibu, and dammit if the car never looked so good. He had a way of making everything around him hotter.

Sighing, I walked around him and opened the backseat door, tossing in my bag.

"What are you doing?" I asked, spinning to face him.

He boxed me in with his body, pressing his palms on either side of the car. My breath hitched at his sudden nearness. *Don't think about how close he is or how wonderfully intoxicating he smells.*

I sank into the cold metal of my car, but it didn't help. My senses went into overdrive. I hadn't been exactly avoiding him, but more or less evading temptation. Damn him and his sexy demon dimples.

"I missed you," he replied in a deep and rich voice that melted over me.

*Be strong. You can resist that smirk.*

"Torent," I groaned, making the mistake of putting my hands on his chest. They were supposed to push him away, yet ignoring the command my brain sent to my hands, they rested over his beating heart. When was I going to accept that I didn't want to avoid Torent or only be his friend?

He grinned, tugging on the end of a frazzled curl. "I love it when you say my name."

I leveled him with a stare that did absolutely nothing to wipe the wickedness from his violet eyes. Tiny flecks of gold were sprinkled in those irises—his demon. I'd only seen Torent lose control once, and although it had been scary, I hadn't been frightened of the darkness that lived within him.

"You're never going to give up the chase, are you?"

"Not when I want something," he crooned.

It was a thrill to hear he wanted me. I couldn't deny the rush his silky words gave me, but I wasn't impulsive or reckless. I'd thought of little else the last few weeks than what my life would be like if I dated a demon.

"What happens when you get bored?" I challenged, although this wasn't the first time we'd had this conversation. It seemed we were doomed to spin circles around each other.

His nose brushed over the tip of mine, bringing our lips too close for comfort. I only had to tilt my head an inch up and I'd be doing the very thing I longed for—kissing the shit out of Torent Stark. One of his hands lifted off the car and trailed down my arm to lace our fingers together. I shocked myself by letting him. In fact, I wasn't sure I could let go.

"Never going to happen, crash car. There's something between us not even I can explain."

"That doesn't make it right."

A gust of wind blew in from the south, and thunder struck over our heads.

"How do you know unless you give us a chance?" His other hand tucked a wayward strand of hair behind my ear, and I shuddered. His body pressed into mine. "I don't know why you insist on resisting this."

*This* being the irrational feelings between us. He was wearing me down. I no longer seemed to remember why I was fighting so hard against what he made me feel. It was exhausting working each day to stay away from him, to not give in to the urge to wrap my arms around him or kiss him brainless in the middle of math class.

He was a distraction.

And there it was. The reason Torent was bad for my health. If I spent all day staring at his gorgeous face, I'd fail all my classes. I'd be stuck in Havenwood Falls with Brooklyn breathing fire down my neck. I'd probably run off and marry him straight out of high school and end up with a dozen equally gorgeous little demon babies.

Sparks lingered at the places his fingers had touched my cheek. Torent, being part demon, could produce a light he called hellfire. I hadn't seen its full potential, but the bits I'd been exposed to were mesmerizing.

"You make me lose myself," I admitted softly.

His focus was completely on me, which was more than a little unnerving. "Why do you see that as a negative thing?"

I angled my face closer to his as if compelled. "I have dreams, plans for my future."

"It doesn't have to be one or the other," he said softly.

Maybe not, but I was afraid of how much I would be willing to give up for him if I let myself, because I knew with certainty that I would fall head over heels in love with him.

This conversation was getting too deep. It was time to divert. "Don't tell me you need a ride. Again."

Torent had used every creative excuse and then some to find time alone with me. It was impossible to not be flattered by his ingenuity . . . or his lingering looks and charming smile.

He gave me a lopsided grin. "The Jeep is in the shop."

"Uh-huh. You need to come up with new material."

His shoulders lifted in a shrug. "Why? This one works so well."

"Get in," I grumbled. I was going to regret this.

He lingered, keeping me pinned to the car with his body. "We're not done talking about you and me. Not by a long shot."

Strolling to the other side of the car, he opened the passenger door.

I exhaled the breath I'd been holding and slid into the driver's seat as he folded himself into my compact vehicle. He made it seem tiny.

Lifting his glorious tush up to one side, he pulled out my brush. "Is this yours?"

I winced, taking the hairbrush he dangled in the air. "Sorry. It was a hectic morning."

Torent relaxed back into the seat. "I heard you were late again."

I tossed the brush into the back of the car and stuck the keys into the ignition, waiting for it to kick over. "Are you keeping tabs on me, Stark?"

His lips twitched as he buckled his seatbelt. "I wouldn't dream of it."

I shifted the car into reverse. "Liar."

He leaned over the center console, fumbling with the radio as I pulled out of the parking spot.

"Are you going to tell me what has you on edge today?" He sounded like he was asking about the weather. "Or am I going to have to seduce it out of you?"

I smacked at the hand that had landed on my thigh. "Don't you dare. I'm driving. Do you really want me to get into an accident?"

He looked so adorable with his jet-black hair disheveled from the wind. "What I want is for you to admit you're enamored by me."

My mouth dropped open. The gall of him! Snapping my mouth shut, I put the Malibu into drive.

"Or . . . you can tell me what's going on," he prodded, as he was so good at doing.

I maneuvered my car in line behind the mass of vehicles trying to exit the parking lot, the weather delaying traffic more than usual. Someone's ball cap flew over the hood of my car and out to the field. I sighed, biting on my lower lip. What could it hurt to tell him the crazy conspiracy theories? It was likely I was worried for nothing. And the worst that would happen was Torent would laugh or tell me I was being silly. I could handle both.

"Beck is convinced I'm cursed. I think Brooklyn is still trying to get revenge on me."

Torent waved at Seth Cooper crossing the parking lot before his eyes ran over me. "Why would you think that? Has something happened?" When I didn't immediately respond, a glint of ominous suspicion sprang into his eyes. "Mallory," he growled so low it caused goose bumps on my arms.

"Geez. Don't get all demon on me. I'm sure it was nothing. I found a bunch of dead birds outside my window this morning."

His fingers brushed at the tiny stubbles under his chin that I found so appealing. The shadow of hair gave him an air of darkness I was clearly attracted to. "Why didn't you tell me?"

Shrugging, I flipped the wheel hand over hand, moving with traffic onto the main road. "I didn't think it was a big deal, but you and Beck are starting to freak me out over it."

Not entirely true. I had already been upset by it this morning, but for some reason, I didn't want to appear weak or superstitious. I didn't want to be that girl who ran to a guy every time she had a problem. I wasn't a damsel in distress who needed to be saved. I had every intention of saving myself.

"Birds often don't die in mass suicides, not in Havenwood Falls."

"I'm learning nothing happens in this town without a reason. I swear, if Brooklyn is still tormenting me because she blames me for taking her powers, I'm going to staple her ass to a chair." The thing was, with my abilities, I could very well carry out the threat.

The muscle along his jaw worked. "Let me talk to her."

"No!" I shouted, nearly swerving off the road. "Don't do that. It would only make things worse. I can deal with her on my own terms."

Torent scowled, either at my driving or at my refusal of his help. "Do you remember what happened the last time you faced off with Brooklyn?"

Did I ever. She nearly killed me. "How could I forget?"

"All the more reason you need to let me find out if she is behind this," he insisted.

"Do you think that's a good idea? You know how touchy she is about us. I don't want to push her and have crap escalating."

"So you're saying there is an *us*?" Torent's eyes twinkled.

How did our conversations always derail so quickly? It was an impressive skill. My lips formed a straight line. "Focus. We were talking about Brooklyn."

Some of the humor dried up, and he got serious. "Go out with me on Saturday."

*Oh, my God. I give up.* I was done fighting him. "Why would I do that?"

He leaned closer, and his fingers twirled a strand of my hair. "Because it would be fun. You remember fun, don't you, Mal?"

Okay, so Torent wasn't the only one with creative excuses. Mine just happened to always revolve around me studying or doing homework. But he had a point. I hadn't gone out in weeks, not even for coffee, and that was just a sin in my book. Locking myself up in the house was not me—it wasn't how I wanted to live. "If I say yes, will you stop asking? One date and that's it."

His lips twitched into a half smile. "One is all it will take."

I shook my head, trying to keep my eyes on the road.

"You really need to work on your confidence," I said dryly. The sky chose that moment to open up, letting the icy rain pour. It plummeted from the black clouds, hitting my windshield with a pattering force that made visibility dodgy. "What is this, the apocalypse?" I'd lived in Wisconsin. I was no stranger to winter, but this was nasty to the tenth degree.

"Maybe we should pull over until the storm passes?" Torent suggested, his eyes narrowing at the ominous clouds above us.

My fingers clenched on the steering wheel. "If I didn't know better, I'd swear you planned this."

He chuckled. "Controlling the weather is unfortunately not one of my skill sets."

I was slowly inching the car along the road and was seriously considering pulling over as Torent had advised. "But you have friends—"

*What the hell?*

A dark shadow was sailing straight at me, and I had no time to react, only brace myself for impact.

*Whack!*

I gave a yelp, my heart roaring in my ears. Something had hit the windshield. I stomped on my brakes, hitting a patch of black ice, and my car spun in a circle. Talk about déjà-freaking-vu.

# CHAPTER 3

*I* don't know how he did it, but Torent took control of the wheel as it spun. It felt as if the car would never stop. A scream lodged in my throat just as he was able to straighten out the wheels and land us in the ditch, narrowly avoiding a massive pine tree.

Torent quickly turned to me, his fingers sliding under my chin to glance over my face. "Are you okay?"

My hands were attached to the steering wheel in a death grip. "I will be as soon as I swallow my heart back down to my chest."

"You're not hurt?" he asked again.

"I-I don't think so . . . but my car," I groaned, staring at the massive spider crack that fissured over the entire windshield in a jagged pattern.

"It's nothing that can't be fixed," he said, trying to downplay the situation.

I failed to mention I had no money, and I hated to ask my Mom. She just started a new job, and there were bills that had to be paid, thanks to her latest divorce. I killed the engine, needing a few moments to collect myself and figure out what I was going to do next. The icy rain was still coming down in buckets.

He surveyed the damage.

"There's a reason I call you crash car," he said, sounding amused. My head hit the back of the seat.

"Not funny. Did you see what it was?" I asked, unclear what I'd hit or what had hit me. The details were fuzzy.

Dark brows furrowed together. "It looked like a small dog."

"What? I hit someone's *dog*?" I shrieked, my heart dropping into my chest. Had I killed a family's dog? I couldn't live with that. This was turning out to be the day from hell.

"It could have been a fox," he added, changing his initial guess, probably to make me feel better. It wasn't working.

"You've got to be shitting me." Unease spread through me like a weed choking the life out of me.

Torent lifted up in his seat, scouring the area surrounding us. "Whatever it was, it's gone."

But was it hurt? Bleeding? Dying alone in the woods?

"You're shaking," he said, gruffness moving into his voice.

I hadn't even realized it until Torent brought it to my attention. Light tremors racked through me. He took my fingers in between his, and a yellow-orange light emitted from his palms, warming up my skin.

"Twice in one day is not a coincidence," I muttered.

"No, it's not."

"What's happening?"

"I wish I knew, but we're going to find out. I'm not going to let anything happen to you."

And I believed him. No one made me feel as safe as Torent did, and that spoke more about my feelings than I was ready to admit. Leaning on him would mean he had the power to hurt me . . . to leave. But facing this problem alone would be stupid. I knew so little about the supernatural world. This was *his* world.

"I'm glad you needed a ride."

The smirk I anticipated spread over his lips. "Good, because I'm picking you up tomorrow."

"I can drive myself to school," I insisted. The aftereffects of shock were slowly starting to wear off.

He glanced at the shattered windshield. "Not in this, you can't."

My head angled left and right, trying to see around the spider crack that splintered over most of the driver's side window. He had a point. It was definitely not safe to drive.

He held out his palm. "Hand me the keys. We'll drop it off at the shop, and I'll grab the Jeep."

What would I do without him? The question scared me.

"Thanks," I said, putting the pink puffball attached to my car key in his hand.

He glanced down at the soft poof and then met my eyes with a raised brow of cynicism.

The corner of my lips lifted. "Pink suits you."

"You suit me."

I swallowed. He had to stop saying things like that. "What am I going to do with you?"

"I could think of a few things." The pitter-patter of rain hitting the roof of the car became the only sound as we shared one of those long heated glances that were becoming far too frequent lately.

I could feel myself getting sucked in. It was a spear of lightning that jolted me from the spell of Torent. "All right, Romeo, let's go before a deer or a bear decides to have a wrestling match with the rest of my car."

"I'd pay to see that."

"You'd pay with your life," I countered, reaching for the door handle.

His raspy chuckle was the last thing I heard as I stepped out of the car to switch places with Torent. I squealed at the first drop of freezing rain on my face. Laughing, we passed each other at the front of the car, headlights beaming over the gravel, and made a mad dash to get back inside the comfort of my Malibu.

Inside the car, Torent cranked the heat so we didn't freeze to death.

"I can't believe there are people who actually love winter," I chattered, shaking out my wet hair.

"Are you telling me you're not a snow bunny?" he asked, adjusting the seat to fit his long frame.

It was weird being on the other side of the car, and I hated to admit it, but I liked the look of Torent behind the wheel. He seemed to be able to fit into every part of my life without trying.

Rubbing my hands together in front of the heater, I snorted. "Hardly."

Easing back onto the road, he asked the question rolling around my own head. "Still think it's Brooklyn screwing with you?"

"I honestly don't know. She does have friends in low places. I'm not ruling anything out at this point." I was more afraid of it not being Brooklyn. I had dealt with her animosity before. A new enemy was the last thing I needed.

"You're just making friends all over the place."

I frowned. "I'm a bucket of rainbows and unicorns."

The drive to Havenwood Falls Garage should have only taken a few minutes, but the storm hampered our time. It was a silent drive, with Torent concentrating on the slick road and me stuck in my head. I had a million questions. Mysteries weren't something I enjoyed, not even in my movies or books. I liked to have all the answers and absolutely hated open endings.

Why would a writer do that? Just why?

I exhaled in relief when the garage came into view, and Torent eased my car into the parking lot. Joshua, the owner, was in the garage, and Torent waved at him as we switched vehicles and jumped into Torent's black Jeep. He had the kind of car that would be able to handle any weather Colorado unleashed. I felt ten times safer.

Snapping my seatbelt together, I glanced over my car one last time. We'd been lucky. The accident could have resulted in more than a broken windshield and shaken nerves. My mind relived those terrifying seconds over and over again. I chewed on my nails as the Jeep began to move.

What if the animal I hit was a shifter? It was possible. I didn't know what was going on, but I was officially on the verge of an emotional meltdown, which would undoubtedly send Torent running for the hills.

"Hey, are you going to be okay?" he asked, and I blinked.

The Jeep was rolling into my driveway. I had spaced the entire ride home. I turned to him and gave him a weak smile. "Yeah. I will be."

What a strange day.

"You're going out with me on Saturday," Torent reminded me, reaching out to tuck a piece of damp hair behind my ear.

I flushed. "I haven't forgotten."

His hands returned to the steering wheel, and I instantly missed his touch. "Good. I'll pick you up in the morning."

"Thanks for the ride." His eyes caught mine in a trance that warmed my blood. I sat unmoving. *Get out of the car, Mallory.* Maybe it was because he looked mouthwatering soaking wet. Maybe it was the brush with disaster. Maybe it was because I hadn't kissed him since Halloween night. Or maybe it was because he wasn't expecting it, but before I changed my mind, I leaned over in my seat, invading Torent's space and pressing my lips to his.

At the brush of my mouth against his, something akin to magic rippled along my skin. Waves of it rose inside me until I could hear the crashing of water. A dizzying excitement fluttered within my chest.

Slowly, watching his stunned eyes, I pulled back to whisper in his ear. "See you tomorrow."

His fingers curled into my wet hair. "We're not finished yet." He reclaimed my lips.

Hunger swept through me as I tasted his breath and the cool metal of his tongue ring. My body ached to press against his, and it took every ounce of my willpower to not climb across the seat into his lap.

God, it was so, so much better than I remembered.

When the kiss ended, he left my lips trembling for more, unfulfilled. Unable to believe I had broken my no-kissing-demons rule, I gathered up my stuff and shifted to open the door, only to quickly spin back to face Torent.

"Wait. I just remembered I have class tomorrow night at the Academy."

Torent cocked his head to the side. "Thursday Awakening class. Not a problem. I can swing by and give you a ride. It will give me an excuse to see you."

"Don't get used to it." I exited his Jeep and ran through the frigid rain into the house, feeling as if my feet never touched the ground and wanting more than life itself to be back inside the warmth of his arms.

Dropping my wet book bag in the front entrance, I ditched my shoes and hoodie before heading toward the kitchen. Gigi had something simmering on the stove that made the house smell like cinnamon and chocolate.

"Was that the Stark boy who dropped you off?" she asked, giving me one of her famous knowing smiles. Her long silver hair was braided to one side.

I nodded, my cheeks flaming with color. Had she seen me kiss him? Or more like devour him?

She opened one of the drawers and withdrew a ladle. "What happened to your car?"

I sank into one of the kitchen chairs, watching her pop around the kitchen, her flowing skirt swishing as it stirred with her movements. It was comforting and homey.

"I got into a little accident."

She flipped her eyes in my direction, suddenly alarmed. "Oh, dear. Are you okay?"

"I'm fine," I quickly assured. "It was a freak accident." Or so I desperately wanted to believe. I didn't want to worry Gigi.

"Another wolf dart into the road?" She was teasing me now.

"No," I said slowly. "I think it was a fox this time. Something sprang into my windshield and cracked it to smithereens. Torent took my car to the shop and gave me a ride home."

Lucky for me, she didn't ask for details. Clucking her tongue, she turned back to the stove. "And in such weather. He seems to always be around when you need him."

Wasn't that the truth, but it was the implication in Gigi's voice that gave me pause. If I didn't know better, I'd think she was encouraging a relationship with a demon. "I guess."

"You like him," she said, not beating around the bush. Her forthrightness was one of the reasons we always got along so well, unlike me and Mom. Gigi joined me at the table with two mugs of hot chocolate topped with whipped cream and peppermint shavings.

My hand wrapped around the Santa mug, letting its warmth seep into my still-cold fingers. There was something to be said for living with Gigi. Mom might not have liked it, but I had never felt more at home or happy. Gigi seemed to always know what I needed.

"The jury's still out." I swiped my finger over the mound of whipped cream and licked it off, doing everything in my power to not think about the kiss Torent and I had shared.

"Hmm." Gigi pursed her lips. "You can't always control your heart."

Sipping on the hot cocoa, I folded my right leg underneath my left. "Boys are complicated. Demons are out of my realm."

She threw her head back and laughed. "Don't let your mother's past dictate your future. You deserve to be happy and have fun, Mal. Enjoy every second of your youth."

How did she know I'd been thinking about my mom and her past relationships? It was uncanny. "I know."

We talked about school, how my night classes at the Academy were going, and my powers. But not once did I mention the dead birds that had been sprawled outside my window this morning. I didn't want to worry her more than I already had with the car incident.

When the hot cocoa was gone, I went to my room feeling better about my crazy day. How foolish would I feel if I was wrong or jumping to crazy conclusions? My life had been anything but simple since I'd come to Havenwood Falls. Was I looking for trouble when there was none?

# CHAPTER 4

*T*ucked away near the main waterfalls in town sat Sun and Moon Academy. It was at this exclusive and hidden academy that students with supernatural abilities like me attended classes. Some went full time during the day, but for students who attended the public schools, the Academy provided night classes during the week.

Torent steered his Jeep through the guarded gates and drove up the long stone road flanked by trees on either side. The perfectly manicured yard was blanketed with white snow that twinkled under the numerous stars and the lanterns placed along the driveway.

"How are classes going? Have you accidentally almost killed anyone else?" Torent asked.

He was referring to my first week in class, when I had nearly embedded a pair of scissors into Otis's chest. Thank Goddess for inhuman reflexes. Word spread quickly about the girl with unpredictable affinity to magnetic energy. I had made quite the name for myself, and not in a good way. Making friends after that had been difficult, to say the least.

"Ha. Ha. Ha. Not yet, but you might be my next victim."

"Being your victim doesn't sound that bad." Torent guided the

Jeep around the circular driveway used for drop-offs. When the car halted, he angled toward me and brushed a lock of hair off my cheek. "Try not to stab anyone in the eye tonight."

I couldn't help but notice how frequently he found little ways to touch me. It happened more and more as of late. I gathered my books and notebooks into my arms before we had a repeat of the other night and ended up making out in front of the Academy.

"Is that why they lock up the weapons before I get there?" I quipped.

He chuckled, and I shut the door on the deep sound, but it had a way of staying with me, even as I walked away.

Stone pathways led up to the main entrance, and the heels of my boots clattered on the cold rock. My fingers pinched the lapels of my coat together. *Don't look back. Don't you dare look back at him*, I chanted in my head, and I made it all the way to the door before I gave in, glancing over my shoulder.

His Jeep was idling, and through the passenger window, he winked at me. I didn't bother to see if anyone was around when I flipped him an obscene gesture and turned around smiling.

Strolling through the arched doors and into the interior courtyard, I headed for the Falls Campus. It was the wing closest to the gushing waterfalls. Christmas was only weeks away, and the town had begun displaying its festive décor. That included the Academy, but the means of decorating was a bit different here than in the town square. Leave it to a magical school to use a holiday as a training session. Magic trembled in the halls as I walked by a group of witches who were streaming strands of garland with fairy lights along the archways, no electricity needed—not when you had magic.

Thursday night at Sun and Moon Academy was Awakening Lab, my favorite class. It was there I got to work on honing my magnetic powers.

Monday nights I had basic supe 101 class. The things I learned in there blew my mind. I never imagined so many different kinds of supernaturals were running around in the world. How had I never noticed before? You'd think I would have seen something, just once, but then maybe I had. The mind conjured justifications for the impossible.

Vampires, fae, werewolves, witches, and many, many other types of teens with mystic abilities moseyed down the halls to class and to the library, or hung out in the halls. I came to the Falls Campus wing, where classrooms spanned off the corridor. I hung a right into one of the rooms. Gianna, the instructor's daughter, smiled at me as I took my seat in the third row beside a fae with blond hair and pretty blue eyes.

There were about twenty other students besides me. I had a few minutes to kill, so I flipped through the supernatural bible, as I referred to the thick textbook. It was a guidebook to the different species. I'd already combed the sections about nymphs and demons.

Because so many of us had different skills, we often split up into groups. I pitied the ones that got stuck with me, but I wasn't the most dangerous. Far from it.

Mrs. Augustine glided into the room as if her feet never touched the ground, her black tunic flowing behind her. Dark curls swept off her neck into a waterfall up-do today.

"Good evening." Her voice was radiant with infectious enthusiasm as she dropped off some papers at her desk. Instead of sitting in the chair, she breezed to the front of her desk and sat on top, letting her feet dangle just above the floor. "As many of you are discovering, your abilities can be linked to your emotions. We'll be exploring some ways to control your powers when your feelings get the best of you." She dove into her lecture.

*Mallory*, a deep voice murmured, interrupting my note-taking. It sounded as if he was sitting directly behind me, but that was impossible, considering a pretty girl with bright red hair was in the desk at my back.

I lifted my pen from the notebook as my eyes darted over the room. Was one of the guys playing a trick on me? Telepathy was possible. I just hadn't met anyone who could project thoughts into my head. Concluding I was losing my mind, I tuned back in to the lecture, but it was harder to concentrate. I kept waiting for the voice again.

Eventually, we were divided into pairs to work on our individual powers. My partner was a witch with an affinity to earth. Elise was a little taller than me with beautiful rich sienna hair that reached the middle of her back. She gave me a polite smile, but I could see in her soft brown eyes she would rather be partnered with someone else.

"Hey." I smiled back, hoping it would put her at ease. "I promise not to use you as a pin cushion." I cringed inside. I had wanted to make a joke, but sometimes they sounded funnier in my head.

Lucky for me, Elise giggled and didn't immediately demand a new partner. "You have an extraordinary gift. Is it true you're dating Torent Stark?"

I choked. Were people really talking about us? "Um, it's complicated."

She let out a dreamy sigh. "Half the girls here would like to be complicated with Torent."

Good to know . . . Actually, I didn't want to know. It caused a hot fire to lick inside my belly. I was jealous. The idea of other girls lusting over my demon caused irrational feelings, a dangerous cocktail for a newbie nymph with strong emotional ties to her powers. Bad things happened if I lost my shit.

The pen on the table beside me trembled. I slapped my hand over it.

*Hold on. Did I really think of Torent as* my *demon?*

God, I'd fallen for him. *It's just a high school crush,* I told myself, not feeling better at the idea.

Something in my expression must have given away what was going on inside my head. "You have it bad, huh? Not that I blame you. I'd take any of the Stark brothers."

*So not helping.*

Before I started to become a possessive maybe girlfriend, I suggested Elise start her portion of the lab first. She nodded and went to gather some materials. All around the room my peers practiced honing their skills. Elise came back with a pot of dirt and a package of orchid seeds. Tearing open the paper packet, she put a single seed into a small pot. Then with a wave of her fingers and a few soft spoken words, she lifted her hand, encouraging the plant to grow. And grow it did. No water. No sun. Just magic.

"That is amazing," I commented in awe. The ability to inspire and nurture life seemed so much more important than my gift. My hand reached out to touch the velvety pink petal, but the moment my fingers grazed the plant, the petals turned a nasty shade of black and withered to dust.

*Uh. Holy crap. Please tell me that did not just happen.*

I jerked my hand away, mortified. Half the class gasped.

Elise took a step away from me, staring at me in horror. "You've been touched by death."

I glanced around the room, seeing so many eyes on me, and panicked. "I-I don't know what that means."

Everything metal in the classroom began to wobble. Chairs. Staplers. Screws. If it was metal, it was vibrating. I had begun to grasp the inner workings of my abilities, but tonight all the training of the last few weeks came undone. And I was horrified by my lack of control. Everyone in the room was now staring at me.

"Mallory," Mrs. Augustine softly spoke my name. "Take a deep breath like we practiced."

Deep breaths, my ass. I was past breathing exercises. Hell, I was struggling to get air into my lungs at all. Mrs. Augustine guided me into a chair and gently eased my head forward so the blood rushed downward.

Oh, God. I was having a legit panic attack in class, and the only person I wanted to see was Torent.

After a few minutes, the air going in and out of my lungs returned to normal, as did the surge of my powers. The trembling of metal objects ceased.

I didn't believe it was death that had touched me, but a vengeful nymph who would do just about anything to gain her powers back.

*Damn you, Brooklyn.*

~

"You're not going to believe what I did in my class last night." It was Friday. Beck and I were in study hall.

He scooted his chair closer to me, getting comfortable, the textbooks beside us forgotten. "Oh, do tell. I hope it's juicy."

"Not exactly. Try humiliating."

He rubbed his hands together. "Even better. Dish."

I relayed the events of my incident with the plant. He already knew about my car and Torent coming to my rescue. Beck approved wholeheartedly, declaring Torent my knight in shining armor. Gah. Beck was such a hopeless romantic and soaked up every nice thing Torent did or said.

Sympathy shone on Beck's face. "Between the dead birds, your car, and the death omen from Elise, I'd say you've gotten yourself into a witchy mess."

"So Brooklyn had me hexed?" I concluded, trying to make sense of what was happening to me.

"It's possible," Beck said, tapping his black-painted fingernail against the table, thinking. "But she is going to great lengths for revenge. Brooklyn doesn't like other people to do her dirty work. It wouldn't give her the satisfaction or attention she craves. This feels like something more."

Ugh. I hated to agree. This didn't feel like jealousy or vengeance. It was subtle. Dark. And personal. Had I made another enemy without even realizing it? "So how do I find out for sure?"

"You need a witch or . . ."

"Or what?" I prompted, a weird feeling of dread opening up in my chest.

"Or an immortal," he murmured.

I sunk back, exhaling loudly. "And where would I find one of those?"

I knew a few witches—Elise was one of them, but I wasn't sure I could convince her to help me, especially if it meant breaking the rules.

Beck lifted a single brow. "Actually, you already know one, sort of. It's possible you might be able to summon her."

I edged forward, leaning in close to Beck. "Who?"

"Styx."

"The goddess?" I mulled the idea around in my head, remembering when I had gone into Peacock Lake and awakened the nymph inside me. Beck's idea might be crazy enough to work. Who better to tell me what was happening to me than the goddess who was my ancestor? I knew next to nothing about the scope of her powers or if she would even answer my call, but it was worth a shot. The alternative of doing nothing and letting the stench of death follow me caused a dry lump to form in my throat. "You're a genius, Beck."

He ran his hands through his vibrant blue hair, his chest filled with cockiness. "Hell yes, I am. So when are we going?"

My shoulders dropped as I remembered my promise to Torent. "I have a date tomorrow."

A grin split over Beck's face. "About damn time. The smoldering glances between you were burning everyone within ten feet."

I said nothing to that and steered the conversation back to my dilemma. "You think Torent would be up for a picnic at Peacock Lake?"

Beck angled his head to the side. "For you, doll, he'd drain the lake if it was what you wanted."

Dramatic much? I rubbed at the back of my neck, trying to release the tension that had been mounting there the last week. The motion didn't go unnoticed by Beck.

"You know what would alleviate some of your stress?" he asked, stretching out his long legs under the table.

I was going to regret asking.

"A massage at the spa?" I suggested, because my muscles could use the relief. Tension had its claws in me.

"Sex with Torent," he said matter-of-factly.

I coughed. "How is that going to uncomplicate my life?"

He shrugged. "Beats me, but it would feel damn good."

"And how would you know?" I retorted, squinting my eyes.

The corner of his lips quirked. "Intuition . . . plus, just look at the guy. He screams amazing in bed."

He had me there. For a few moments, I entertained the idea of getting sweaty in between the sheets with Torent. God knew every fiber in my body wanted to do the nasty with the demon.

# CHAPTER 5

*I*t had been snowing on and off all day—just a light dusting, but enough to make Havenwood Falls look like an idyllic shaken snow globe. Torent would be here in thirty minutes for our date, and I was still strutting around my room in nothing but a T-shirt, trying to decide what to wear.

The problem was, Torent and I had very different plans for tonight. How did one dress to summon a goddess? I settled on jeans and a warm knitted sweater in soft teal that brought out the color of my eyes. The doorbell rang as I finished defining my eyes with black liner.

With a long exhale, I left my room and walked down the hall. I heard Torent's deep voice greet Gigi and Mom. When I came down the stairs, the two of them were drilling Torent with questions, but the demon didn't seem to mind. If I didn't know better, I would have said he was enjoying himself, having the attention of Mom and Gigi.

"Am I interrupting?" I asked, standing on the bottom step with my arms crossed.

Mom gave me a crooked smile. "We were just occupying Torent while you finished getting ready."

Her platinum blond hair hung down the center of her back. She wore a dark blue gypsy skirt that fell almost to her bare feet, where a gold chain glittered on her ankle.

I pursed my lips, eyeing the two of them because if I glanced at Torent, they would see just how bad I had it for the demon. "Hmm. I'm sure that's what you were doing."

"I'll make sure to have her home before curfew," he told Mom and Gigi, like he was a saint. He had to be the most polite demon on the planet.

"Be safe. Don't do anything I would do," Mom warned.

I rolled my eyes and mouthed goodbye, closing the door before I sustained further embarrassment. "I'm sorry about that. I had no clue how interested they would be in my dating life."

He opened the passenger door to his Jeep. "At least you finally admit we're dating."

I spun around as I was about to hop into his car. Torent sent me a characteristic look, those direct violet eyes boring into mine. This was that moment I had wanted to avoid inside. That second where our eyes connected and nothing else in the world mattered but him. My heart and stomach turned in twirls. I wanted him to kiss me so badly, I could barely stand it. We hadn't even gotten into the car yet, and I was already melting at his feet.

I swallowed the rapid beating of my heart. "Let me rephrase."

His finger pressed to my lips. "There is no way I'm letting you take it back, crash car."

His smile nearly killed me. If he was going to play wicked, so could I. Licking my lips, my tongue flicked over his finger, and I watched as his eyes darkened, glimmering with flecks of gold.

Making out in my driveway was not what I had in mind for this date. We had to at least get into the car, but if he kept looking at me like that . . .

Flashes of blue, purple, and pink streamed over our heads, drawing my attention. I realized I'd intertwined my fingers with his other hand. The streaks of Northern Lights were a product of our combined powers.

"We should probably go," I whispered. "Before we end up with an audience."

His husky chuckle drifted over me. "Not until I hear you say it."

"That I'm not dating a demon," I retorted, and slipped into the Jeep before he could argue.

Shaking his head, Torent closed the door and made his way around the car.

I settled into the seat, shifting my body so I was turned toward Torent, and fumbled with a piece of yarn from my sweater. "I need to ask a favor."

Torent tensed, the lines on his face deepening. "Normally, I wouldn't hesitate, but there is something in your voice that is giving me pause."

He wasn't the only one, but I pushed forward, trying to make light of what I was going to ask of him. "Don't go all holy on me now."

He ran a hand through his hair. "What kind of favor are you asking for?"

*Here goes nothing.* I didn't know exactly how Torent would react to my request. "I need to go to Peacock Lake."

"Why, exactly?" His chest rumbled. "You know it's freezing out, right?"

The weather wasn't my concern. The dead things that kept happening to me definitely were. "Answers. I need answers, and the only way I can think to get them is to ask the goddess who gave me these blasted powers. Maybe something went awry."

"I'm not sure that's how it works," he declared, sounding more confident than I felt. "The likelihood of a goddess screwing up seems highly doubtful."

I jerked my chin up and attempted to keep the snap out of my voice, but I failed. "Look, I need your help. Are you in or not?"

Couldn't he see how vital this was to me? I had promised him a date, and I refused to go back on my word, but at the same time, this wasn't something I could shrug off. The importance of it stained the air like a dark shadow looming over me.

"If I say no, you're just going to go out on your own." It wasn't a question, but more of him thinking out loud.

I didn't lie. Not to him. "Yes," I agreed.

His dark eyes flicked to mine. "Is it dangerous?"

"Probably," I replied with equal coolness, then jumped to plead my case. "I know this wasn't what you had planned for tonight, but I think it is important I go. I'll make it up to you." I was so going to regret that promise, but every bone in my body was telling me I needed to go to the lake. It was there I would get the answers I sought . . . I prayed.

His grin was slow and daring. "How can I say no to a little danger? And if it gets me another date with you, I'm in."

The air was chilly on my nose and cheeks as I pulled my coat closer in around me. *Why hadn't I thought to bring a hat or gloves?* With the sun gone, the temperatures had plummeted.

My boots crunched through the frozen grass. I matched my strides with Torent's, having to take twice as many steps to keep up with him. Trees surrounded us from all sides, their branches and leaves glistening under the moon and canopy of stars.

Noticing I was lagging behind, he slowed down and reached for my hand, interlacing our fingers. A flare of light burst from the center of his palm, sending a stream of warmth into our joined fingers.

"Are you sure this is a good idea?" he asked for the third time.

I nearly sighed at the heat of his hellfire. A hug would be amazing. "No, but I don't see what other choice I have."

The closer we got to the lake, the faster my heart raged in my chest, in my throat. We were getting close. A tingle of both excitement and terror tiptoed down my—

A wolf howled through the trees. I automatically moved closer to Torent.

"Maybe we should have brought Beck," I murmured. These woods were filled with all types of shifters, among other things.

His arms tightened around me, and he tipped his nose to look down at me with a raised brow. "You don't think I can protect you?"

"I didn't say—"

A blur of color sped past us, kicking up grass and dirt. I stiffened in his arms, my heart racing like a gazelle.

"Did you see that?" I asked in a whispered hiss. A brush of ice slunk across the nape of my neck, but Torent didn't seem as concerned.

His body stayed warm and relaxed against mine. "It was just a vamp out hunting."

My mouth dropped open. "Just a vamp?" I shrilled, my voice echoing over the treetops. "And a hungry one at that."

"Relax. We're not going to be dinner. Demon blood is not very appetizing."

"What about nymph blood?"

The curve of his lips was immoral. "Oh yeah, you're a delectable five-course meal."

"Torent," I hissed, frustration coating my voice.

His hands landed on my shoulders as he leaned down to gaze directly into my eyes. "This was your idea, but you have nothing to fear. I won't let anything happen to you. I promise."

Ensnared by the mixture of violet and gold in his eyes, I exhaled. Why did he have to say things like that? I nodded, afraid my voice would give away the plethora of feelings he sent off inside me.

In the distance, my ears picked up a gentle hum of music, like a lullaby beckoning me.

"We're almost there," I murmured, stepping away from Torent toward the sound.

I barely knew these woods, had only been here once, but I knew if I closed my eyes, I would be able to find Peacock Lake without even trying. We had a connection, the lake and I.

It was only a few more minutes of trekking through the woods before we came upon Peacock Lake. A fine mist swirled over the slightly frozen pond. A thin layer of ice blanketed the surface, shining like glass. The small waterfall trickled over stone and a hum of lovely voices called me to the water.

Entranced, I slowly walked toward the edge of the lake. Torent stopped me, encircling his hands around my waist. "Whoa. You can't go in there, Mal. The water is ice."

"It's okay. I won't feel the coldness of the water. Nymph thing," I assured, going with my gut. When my hand grazed the surface, I felt nothing but welcome.

His voice grew tight, and I sensed his eyes on me. "I guess we all have our thing, but I would feel better if you let me help, just to be sure."

I couldn't mistake the concern I heard. He was worried, and I couldn't blame him.

It was a struggle to pull my gaze from the water and look at Torent. The pull to submerge myself in the lake was strong. I didn't know how long I could hold off. "Suit yourself."

I slipped off my boots. Torent came to the edge beside me and crouched down. He dipped his hand into the frigid water, and I watched in fascination as his eyes turned the color of melted gold and his fingers glowed with hellfire. The light spread through the depths of the glassy lake, from one side to the other, encompassing it completely. White steam billowed higher, lowering visibility. He leaned forward, the gold in his irises brightening.

My eyes narrowed as something in the water captured them. A dark phantom shadow rose from the bottom straight for Torent. Panic clawed in my chest for a split second. I grabbed his arm and yanked him back. "Not so close."

Something about the lake wanted Torent, sort of in the same way I did . . . but more—to possess him. I had sensed its desire in my soul. There were things that lurked in the small lake, things I didn't understand and wasn't sure I wanted to.

If he thought my attitude suddenly strange, he didn't let on. Perhaps he had sensed the power of this place as I did.

"That should keep you from freezing to death," he said quietly.

Because I had forgotten to bring a change of clothes, I slipped out of my jeans and sweater, leaving me in a tank top and my undergarments. My teeth chattered as I stepped one foot and then the other into the shallow part of the lake. I spun around to look back at Torent. "Don't go far."

His eyes blazed, the muscle at his jaw tightening. It was clear from his expression he wished I would come back to shore. This was possibly one place Torent couldn't save me. "I'm not going anywhere without you, crash car."

I gave him an encouraging smile for both our sakes and made an impulsive decision I hoped would ease some of his tension. I blew him a kiss and went under.

Water caressed my face like silk. I was calmer than I imagined. It was the lake. The idea of summoning a goddess underwater should have caused considerable anxiety.

I swam sure and strong, going deeper into the dark blue lake. And like the first time, it called to me, a gentle song I had to answer with my own.

When the light in the water began to change, I hovered, the song growing louder around me. My lungs worked effortlessly underwater as if I'd grown gills, a freaky thought. I wasn't sure what to do next or what to say, so I opened my mouth and called her name.

"Styx. I need your help."

The water surrounding me was mesmerizing—the lethal, gentle beauty of such power. I waited. And waited. I listened to the serene quiet, but no divine response came. Instead, a bead of light formed below my dangling feet. It soared toward me, enhancing until I was nearly blinded by its brightness. It encased me from all sides.

Then I heard her voice, clear and powerful. "I know why you've come, daughter, and this is what I can offer you."

The light swirled, and from the ribbons of water and magic, images formed. My hand reached out and went through the projection, rippling the vision. Within seconds, I was sucked into the past.

# CHAPTER 6

*man with sand-colored hair crept through the trees like a lurker. Beyond the thick woods in front of him was a clearing where a group gathered, one of them being my mother. She looked so young and yet so much the same. A shadow of sorrow and fear cloaked her eyes as the four of them formed a circle, two other women and a young man. None of them looked much older than me.*

*My eyes volleyed between the tree line and the clearing. I couldn't shake the feeling that something bad was about to happen. The air seemed to tremble with fear and anger.*

*The four joined hands, and a woman with dark hair began to chant. Her voice didn't carry as I had hoped. I had to stretch to try to understand her words, picking up only bits and pieces of what I believed was a spell.*

*My education on witchcraft was measly, so even what I heard didn't make sense. I couldn't decipher what sort of spell she was performing, but I got the feeling it was important.*

*The witch lifted her face to the stars, color spilling over her porcelain cheeks. "Watchers and guardians of the elements, I ask for a shard of your powers—"*

*Her voice was carried away by a gust of wind, leaving me on the cusp of the clearing still clueless as to what was happening, but one thing was certain—the lurker was about to make a move.*

*I opened my mouth to warn my mother, but a flash of silvery moonlight hit the man's face, and I gasped. Recognition speared through me. I knew that face. Not from a single memory, but from a photograph.*

*He was my father.*

*What was he doing here?*

*Maybe I had it wrong? Perhaps he was here to help my mother.*

*But a few moments later that theory was blasted out of the water.*

*My father struck out with a spell of his own, his voice bellowing over the glade. The circle disbanded, and pleas were exchanged, but my mother wasn't able to dissuade my father. His eyes hardened, filling with such rage, it caused the hairs on my arms to stand up.*

*A flash of light hurled from the brown-haired witch, and the air filled with screams. My father, a mage or sorcerer with superior skills, reacted with magic of his own. My vision was impaired by the brightness of the magic. I couldn't see what was happening, only hear the horrible cries and the dead silence that followed. When my eyes adjusted, the body of the young man who had been part of the circle lay awkwardly on the ground, his blood seeping into the earth and my father towering over him.*

The vision dispelled, leaving only the murky depths of the blue waters. Styx appeared, her hair floating around her like a halo of darkness. "You, my daughter, will suffer the sins of your blood."

Well, shit. That sounded dreadful.

"What sins? What had my father done?" I asked, feeling like I had more questions than answers.

Her cloak of pure white gleamed in the water like a ray of hope. "There is some magic that binds to your bloodline, including the hex bestowed upon your father. When you awakened, you also activated that blood hex within yourself, as his only living heir."

Fucking fabulous. I'd never met the man who helped create me, yet it was his past that haunted me. Sometimes parents sucked.

"How do I break it?" I asked, doing my best to keep calm and not let the surge of panic draw me under.

Her white eyes dimmed, growing sad. She didn't have to tell me what I already knew. Not even a goddess had all the answers. "That is your burden to bear, for blood magic is not of my realm, but you *must* stop death from consuming you."

"I don't know how," I said softly.

"I'm sorry, daughter. You must go." Her arms swept through the water, not giving me the chance to drill her with the millions of questions jumbled inside my head. She created a wave of water that lifted me upward.

I broke through the surface, sucking in a sharp bite of air that scored my throat, and stared into Torent's dark eyes.

"Christ, Mallory," he swore, dragging me against him. "I swear to God, you ever do that to me again and I'll drown you myself."

Shivering against his chest, I threw my arms around him and clung to his neck. "I'm sorry," I shuddered.

Fear and something close to anger smoldered in his gaze. "I thought you drowned."

We were wading in the edge of the lake, the moon shining high over our heads.

"I'm okay." *As long as you keep holding me,* I said to myself. But we both must have wanted the same thing, because his arms never let go as he led us out of the water to the rocky shore. "I saw my father," I said after a few heartbeats.

"In the lake? You had a vision?"

I nodded. "Styx gave it to me."

His hand reached out for me, and I shivered as he brushed cool wet fingers along my cheek. "Did she give you the answers you were searching for?"

Tears welled up in my eyes. I was on the verge of losing it. My bottom lip trembled.

"Shit. I got you," he murmured, engulfing me in his arms a second time. His hellfire flared to life, keeping me warm from the night's chill.

An onslaught of emotions came barreling at me, and I could no longer fight them off. Leaning into Torent, I let him be the strong one, dropping the walls around me and letting the tears come. They racked through my body, shaking my shoulders. It suddenly felt like I had lost control of my life. Just like that. Nothing made sense. Not who I was. Not who my parents were. And at the same time, it all made sense. Why Mom had left. Why we had never come back. What she had been running from—protecting me from.

It was only a few minutes that I allowed myself to wallow in self-pity. Drying up the tears, I pulled back and glanced up into Torent's face. I bit my lip. "I didn't mean for that to happen."

The hand he had moved into my hair came to settle on my cheek, brushing at the dampness. "Come on, let's get you home. You can tell me what happened on the way."

Did I have the strength to tell him what I had seen without the waterworks boiling up a second time? Torent squeezed my hand, and I realized with him at my side, I had more strength then I'd ever had in my life. He gave me courage and fortitude.

We hiked back through the woods fairly quickly. I had finished relaying all that I had seen and heard while I'd been in Peacock Lake as we emerged from a cluster of pine trees.

"My girlfriend is hexed. We make quite the pair, you and I," he said, grabbing my hand to cross the road to his car.

My lips turned down, and I tried to wiggle my fingers out from his, but he wasn't letting go. "I'm not your girlfriend."

"It's only a matter of time," he added with a shit-eating grin.

Leave it to Torent to make me forget about the blood hex for even the briefest amount of time. He would know exactly what to say to get under my skin.

We approached his Jeep, and I was more than ready to go home, but before I could reach for the door handle, I found myself pressed up against the cool metal of the car, Torent's firm body capturing me there. My heart raced at blinding speed, and I cursed him for making me feel like this.

"Don't you ever scare me like that again." His fingers were on my wrists, thumb pressed against the inside of my pulsing vein.

"It was never my intention. I just wanted answers." Answers I still didn't have, but Styx had given me something to start with, and it was more than I had an hour ago.

He idly traced circles up my forearm. I breathed in the scent of him, earthy and crisp. The combination of his touch and smell caused my stomach to flip.

"I make you nervous," he murmured, his lips hovering so close to my cheek his hot breath rushed over my skin. "This thing between us scares you."

Lifting my lashes, I met his smoldering eyes. "And it doesn't you?"

"You should be a little afraid. You bring out the darkness inside me." Gold flecks brightened in the center of his irises, and I saw he was on the verge of losing control, but the problem was, I was right there with him.

His lips came down on mine, not soft or gentle, but with a passion that made my heart burst. Did I feel this connection to Torent because we both had something dark and evil in our souls? If that was so, should we be embracing or running from each other? I didn't know, didn't have the answers. All I had was this moment and how he made me feel. Beautiful. Powerful. Desired. Loved.

He broke off the kiss as swiftly as he took my lips, leaving me gasping and aching for more. My hands struggled against the hold he still had on my wrists, dying to dive into his hair and pull him back for more. He was taunting me. His tongue traced my lips, and I shivered, feeling the cool metal of his piercing against my mouth. He took a lazy journey along the column of my throat, sparking electricity wherever he kissed.

I sighed when he released one of my hands to trace the pad of his thumb over my bottom lip.

"Open for me," he whispered, reclaiming my mouth, but this time, his tongue swooped in.

My entire world fell off balance, and I was spinning wildly out of control. His fingers intertwined with both my hands, and I squeezed, holding onto him for dear life.

Ending the kiss, he murmured thickly, "I want to be anywhere right now other than here." A pause lingered in the air between us. "Get in the car. I need to take you home."

It was probably a good thing we weren't somewhere else. With my emotions all mixed up, I didn't have the energy to refuse what my body and heart clearly wanted. One thing was certain. I wanted Torent. That hadn't changed.

# CHAPTER 7

*T*he house was dark and silent when I got home. Nothing stirred. Feeling like an emotional basket case, I tiptoed to my room, looking for solitude to sort out what I'd learned, besides the fact that I was falling wholeheartedly in love with a demon.

That was a problem for another night.

After stripping out of my grimy clothes, I flopped down on my bed, telling myself I wasn't going to have another pitiful-me moment. For so long, mystery swirled around the man who was my father, but tonight I discovered he was a mage, a detail no one had bothered to share. His aspiration for power had led him down a dark path—the darkest.

Although I hadn't inherited his power, I had inherited his blood hex.

I needed more information about that night. Who was the man my father had murdered with his spell? I had a hunch, but I needed facts. Mom would have been the most accurate source, but she had gone to great lengths to keep this from me. Something told me she wasn't going to be extremely forthcoming with the details.

Did she know about the repercussions of that night? About the blood curse? I didn't know if I was more afraid to find out she did or didn't. Either way, she had hidden this from me, had lied to me.

Thinking about the man I never got the chance to understand and only dreamt about caused my heart to tighten. Abandonment was a strange thing, inducing emotions that appeared in sporadic patterns. At this point in my life, I rarely thought about the man who fathered me. He had become only a tiny piece of my past that was better left in the past. I did have those few days a year I wallowed, becoming a little girl who wanted nothing more than to see her father . . . just once. Then I'd stepped foot into Havenwood Falls, and it seemed the past was determined to taint my future.

I had so many questions, most of them not good.

As a child, I learned to stop seeking those answers from Mom. Seeing how upset they made her was enough to have me biting my tongue. I hated to cause her sadness, and it was evident my father was the source of deep scars that had never healed.

Rolling over, I swung my feet off the bed to grab my laptop. Time to slap on my cryptic detector. If there was one thing my generation had skills at, it was the Internet.

I slunk behind my desk and opened my computer. It was amazing what you could find on the web—and truly frightening at the same time. When the Google homepage came up, I took a deep breath and typed in his name.

*Roth Dorian.*

How many times had I searched his name over the Internet? A hundred at least, but not once did I get a hit on a Roth Dorian from Havenwood Falls. Why would this time be any different?

Except . . . it was.

My heart beat triple time in my chest at the results scrolling down the screen. Headlines from the Sun & Moon Tribune popped out at me, causing a sick twist in my stomach. A part of me wanted to believe the vision had been false—a lie. My father couldn't possibly be a murderer, because if he was, what would that mean for me? Did that mean I was truly doomed?

I mulled over the words on the screen:

**Breaking news. Family seeks answers after the mysterious death of their son.**

**One dead in an apparent murder, rocking the small town of Havenwood Falls.**

**Roth Dorian convicted of murdering his best friend.**

Local news had chronologically documented the events. Something or someone in Havenwood Falls had kept it from leaking out. It was the only explanation, which meant it was definitely supernatural causes that had killed . . .

What had been his name—the poor guy my father had chosen to play God with?

I clicked on one of the headlines, skimming through the text. It was dated six months from the month and year I was born. His name jumped off the screen, and my temples started throbbing. It couldn't be.

Ryle Kendall.

Suddenly pieces of the puzzle were fitting together. I'd stake my nymph powers on Ryle being related to Brooklyn and the root of the rift between our families. Who could blame them? My father had murdered someone they loved, but just who had Ryle Kendall been?

Scrolling further down, a picture caught my eye. I gaped at my father's image from over eighteen years ago. Seeing the man who was responsible for my creation made my belly tangle in knots. He had changed from the single picture Mom had tucked away in a keepsake box. I used to sneak into her room and climb into the back of the closet, playing with the trinkets and staring at the smiling man with his arm around Mom. They had seemed so young and happy in that second captured by film.

But in his mug shot from that horrific day, he appeared older, harder, and cynical. His auburn hair was disheveled. Long lashes surrounded vibrant green eyes, no longer twinkling with lightheartedness. I had his slim nose and almond-shaped eyes. It was weird staring at him and seeing parts of myself.

*Murderer. Murderer. Murderer.*

The word stared back at me as if it was flashing in neon lights, bold and bright on every screen.

With an exasperated oath, I snapped my laptop closed and faced the view outside my window—tall oak and aspen trees towered toward the sky, glittering with a dusting of white snow.

I toyed with the end of my braid. My father had killed Brooklyn's relative. No wonder her family hated mine. I couldn't believe Mom had any involvement. She wouldn't have.

This had to be the reason she had run from Havenwood Falls.

∽

I spent the rest of the weekend stressing over what I was going to do with the information I'd learned. Torent texted me a few times to check on me. I was grateful for his support. Dealing with this on my own would have sucked.

Multiple times on Sunday I tried to work up the nerve to talk with Mom, ask her what had happened that night, but the right time never came up. Or maybe it was me. Maybe I wasn't ready.

Monday came before I knew it, and I realized who I needed to talk to. It wouldn't be easy, but she could fill in some of the remaining holes.

I was dreading lunch, knowing it was the only time to corner Brooklyn. My stomach twisted like a pretzel, and I was positive I wouldn't be able to eat without hurling.

Taking a seat at my usual table, my knee whacked into the edge, and I swore. My nails scraped against my teeth as I chewed on them, watching Brooklyn strut into the cafeteria like she was queen. She liked to make an entrance and was often the last to arrive, which only prolonged the nerves scrambling inside me.

Beck snuck up behind me. "Why do you look like the green hot dogs they serve on Wednesday?" He slid into the chair next to mine.

I gritted my teeth. "Because I feel like one."

He raised a brow.

"I have to talk to Brooklyn," I explained with anguish.

A grim expression crawled onto his face. "Do you have a death wish?" he hissed.

"Today, I do." Staring at the table where Brooklyn and her

sidekicks, Leena and Cora, were sitting, I drew in a breath. Stalling was my specialty. Instead of stalking straight up to her and unleashing what I had on my chest, I quickly gave Beck a rundown of my date with Torent.

"That is some serious family baggage." He ran a hand through his blueberry-colored hair. "Do you really think you're hexed?"

"I don't want to believe it, but there is definitely something happening to me."

"God, this is so messed up. You're too nice of a person to be cursed by something your father did."

I rubbed my eyes, suddenly bone tired. "Thanks."

Beck glanced over at Brooklyn's table with wary eyes. "Good luck," he whispered and patted me between my shoulder blades. "I got your back if shit goes south."

I hoped it didn't come to that. The last thing I wanted was another confrontation with Brooklyn in front of the school. Forgoing food, I grabbed a vanilla shake and weaved my way through the cluster of tables toward the center of the cafeteria. Brooklyn and her friends always sat in the same spot, the table directly in front of the large window.

Brooklyn saw me immediately. She was chatting with Leena and Cora, twisting her midnight hair around her finger. Cora laughed at something Brooklyn said, but Brooklyn's lips puckered when I stopped at their table. She narrowed her dark blue eyes. Everything about Brooklyn reminded me of an untamed tsunami, and for a second, I thought about turning around and leaving.

*No.*

I would solve nothing by chickening out and hiding in my room, pretending the problem didn't exist. Things would only get worse. The only way to break this blood hex was to find out more about its origin, and I needed Brooklyn to do that.

My nails tapped on the table. "Mind if I join you?"

"Yes, I do mind," Brooklyn snapped. "We don't associate with trash."

I had expected nothing less than a cold welcome from my fellow nymph. Ignoring her ill behavior, I plopped my ass into the seat beside Leena, not caring if I pissed her off. She was already always angry with me. The entire room went on edge, wondering what would happen next. Our complicated relationship was no secret at school, so the stares and whispers were expected. I glanced at Brooklyn, Cora, and Leena. The four of us were nymphs. We should have been friends, but circumstances made that impossible.

And that was why I was here.

I wanted to know what information Brooklyn had. She might be able to fill in all the holes about that night, and with any luck, she would know something about the blood hex, but I needed to be careful. The last thing I wanted was for Brooklyn to use it against me somehow.

"I need your help," I stated, meeting her directly in the eyes.

Brooklyn threw her head back and laughed. "That's rich. Why would I ever help you?" Her voice had grown louder.

My stomach clenched, but I forced my lips into a half smile. "You're going to make a scene, huh?"

Leena and Cora had become very interested in their salads. I couldn't blame them. Brooklyn had a way of drawing attention, even negative attention.

She flipped her hand over, examining her hot-pink-painted nails. "Is there a time I don't?"

My chest heaved. "Fine. Let me get to the point. We've already established you hate me. I'm not looking to be BFFs. I have some questions."

Her eyes hardened. "You've got five minutes before I give you the shock of your life."

She wasn't kidding. Brooklyn would be the kind of supe who wouldn't care about rules. No magic in front of humans, so it would be wise to heed her warning.

"You said my father was evil. I know he was convicted of murdering someone in your family," I said, getting straight to the point. I didn't have time to beat around the bush.

Leena and Cora both let out audible gasps, hands flying to their mouths. I took it Brooklyn hadn't told her besties about the strife between our families.

The expression on her pretty face could have been construed as impressed—or maybe it was haughtiness. It was hard to tell. "I can't believe it has taken you so long to figure out. He was my uncle, my father's brother. I was deprived of knowing him, thanks to *your* father."

I didn't think this would be easy, but Brooklyn was going to make it worse than swallowing a mouthful of bile. "Looks like we have more in common than either of us would like."

She scoffed. "I'm nothing like you."

"Whatever. I didn't have time to make you a list, and I don't want to argue. What I want to know is if you have any information on what happened that night."

Her dainty shoulders shrugged. Brooklyn loved nothing more than having the knowledge I wanted. It gave her an edge. But she surprised me by divulging information. "Only what I've been told, that your father was a power-hungry warlock who turned to the dark side. His dabbling in black magic corrupted his heart and soul. My mom and my uncle, who was a year younger, had been friends with your mother. When your mom noticed things had changed inside your father, she wanted to leave him and turned to my mom for help. Your mother knew your father wouldn't let her go easily, especially if he found out she was pregnant, which he had. The three of them sought the help of a witch to perform a spell that would sever any ties with your father, including memories of your mom being pregnant."

A nasty sinking feeling settled in my stomach. What Brooklyn was saying coincided with the vision. My heart hurt for my mother and what she must have been going through. But my heart broke for the boy who lost his life that night.

Everyone around the table was on the edge of their seats, including me, waiting to hear what happened next. Brooklyn might be a raging lunatic, but she wasn't a half bad storyteller. Who would have thought?

"The night they gathered with the witch to perform the spell, your father showed up. He broke their circle. My uncle lunged, and his heroic actions to protect *your* mother cost him his life. Your father hit him with a death spell," she spat, her voice growing in anger.

Maybe this wasn't such a good idea. She seemed to be getting heated over the retelling. "I'm sorry, Brooklyn, but you have to know that has nothing to do with me."

"You're wrong. It has everything to do with you. It was because of you," she barked in a thin voice.

If I snapped back, I wouldn't get any more details from Brooklyn. I had to rein the growl back and remain calm.

"What happened . . . after?" I asked as smoothly as I could manage.

Crossing her arms over her chest, Brooklyn glared at me. "They locked your father up."

My life had become something out of a paranormal novel. Hell, my life was a paranormal murder mystery.

Her head tilted to the side as she continued to glower at me. "They said he went mad in prison. You're going to end up just like him," she hurled with venom strong enough to poison me.

Did she—? Had she—? I couldn't even grasp the implication behind her words. I got it. She hated me and had more reason to hate me than anyone else. But me? Murder someone? Was that the curse? Was I doomed to kill someone? Torent? Beck? Brooklyn? Okay, the last idea I could entertain for a hot minute, but no matter how ugly Brooklyn could be, I would never have the heart to end her life.

But throw a milkshake at her?

Hell yes.

Something inside me snapped. It happened so fast, a gut reaction. Before I got the chance to process what my hand was doing, the vanilla shake clutched in my fingers was sailing across the table. The semiliquid ice cream splattered down the front of

Brooklyn's shirt. Poor Cora, who was sitting next to Brooklyn, caught some of the stray drops.

I had assaulted the mean girls with a milkshake.

"You basic bitch," Brooklyn seethed, jumping to her feet. Flames radiated in her eyes.

"Oops," I said with a sly smile, a hand flying to my lips. Things just got a little messy. This wasn't going to bode well for my social status.

"You'll pay for this." Brooklyn's voice had gone so low, prickles formed at the back of my neck.

Wasn't I already?

# CHAPTER 8

*I* ran from the lunchroom. Someone called my name over the cafeteria chatter. I thought it was Beck, but I kept going, quickly turned the corner, and smacked into Torent. I swear the demon had ESP when it came to me. He had a way of always being in the right place at the right time. The universe was telling me something, and I was being too stubborn to listen.

His hands landed on my shoulders, preventing me from bolting. "Hey, what's wrong? You look like you've seen a ghost."

"I need to go home," I rushed out, trying to maneuver around him a second time, but he wasn't having it.

His fingers stayed firm on my shoulders. "Fine, I'll drive you."

"There's no point in us both getting detention for skipping class." I could sense the metal around me—the lockers, the screws in the walls, and the supports under the floor—but the school's wards kept me from going full metal freak-out. Otherwise, I might have very well brought the school walls down around me.

The idea was terrifying, but the dark shadow of thoughts in my head petrified me more.

What if Brooklyn was right? What if I was as dark as my father? What if the combination of being the daughter of the goddess of night and a warlock doomed me to an ill-omened fate?

His hands trailed down my arms, and he interlaced our fingers, giving them a squeeze. "You're worth giving up a Saturday for."

I nodded. No arguments this time. I needed to get out of here.

Torent drove us out of the school parking lot toward my house in silence. I stared out the window at the snow-covered mountains rolling by. The view was always beautiful in Havenwood Falls and with Christmas just a few weeks away, the town looked like something out of a painting with its colored lights, bright red bows, and handcrafted pine wreaths, but today I barely noticed. My mind glazed over the landscape, stuck in my own thoughts.

"Are you going to tell me what happened?" Torent asked, breaking me out of my trance.

I pulled my gaze from the side window to look at him. He had the kind of dark beauty a girl could easily get hung up on. "Only if you promise not to laugh."

He took a hand off the steering wheel for a second and held it up in a salute. "Demon's honor."

I snorted. A demon's honor meant crap, but this was Torent, and I had come to trust him as much as I did Beck. "I threw a milkshake at your ex-girlfriend."

His lips twitched. "I would have paid to see that. Any chance I could get you to do it again?"

Crossing my arms, I sank down in the seat. "I'm sure it's already up on YouTube."

"What did she say to piss you off?"

He knew Brooklyn well and how she loved to push my buttons. Being short-tempered and on edge didn't help the situation. I was angry, along with a shit ton of other emotions. "She can be such a heinous bitch."

"Very true," he agreed, keeping his focus on the road.

"She isn't entirely to blame," I admitted, even though the admission left a bad taste in my mouth. "I don't know what I was thinking, going to her for information, but she did fill in some missing gaps about my father and what happened that night."

His lips turned down into a frown. "And that's what has you running?"

I wasn't running, was I?

Maybe a little, but more than anything I wanted my mom.

It was time she and I had a little chat. No more secrets. No more lies. I deserved the truth. I wasn't a child to be protected any longer.

I walked through the front door and was overwhelmed with a sense of nostalgia. I hadn't grown up in this house, but over the month it had become my home and represented everything I had ever longed for. Stability. Love. Roots.

My boots shuffled over the hardwood floors into the family room, where I found my mom curled up on the couch with a book. The fireplace was roaring, wood popping and crackling in the stone hearth. She looked so beautiful with the glow of amber highlighting her golden skin and hair. Today was her day off from work.

"Mom?" My voice was soft but carried over the room.

She jumped, the trashy romance book she had been engrossed in falling into her lap. "Mallory, you scared me." Her eyes glanced over the clock on the wall before her brows furrowed together in confusion. "What are you doing home? Shouldn't you be in school?"

I tried to keep the tears at bay as I walked to the couch. She pulled her feet in closer so I could sit.

"Honey, what's got you so upset?" she asked, placing the book from her lap onto the coffee table.

The words came pouring out. "Why did you never tell me my father was a murderer?"

She wasn't shocked by what I said, not like I imagined she would have been. The only reaction on her face was a slight lift of her eyes, but the few moments of silence spoke volumes. "I'll make us some coffee. We could both use it. And then we'll talk."

I was grateful for a minute or two to collect myself. She came from the kitchen with two mugs, offering me one before sitting back down beside me on the couch.

Lifting her feet up on the rectangular table, she stared into the fireplace. "I've dreaded this moment since the day you were born. It was foolish of me to have taken you from Havenwood Falls. I see that now, but back then, I was scared and desperate to save you from a fate not of your making. I wanted more than anything to give you the life of your choosing, but some things can't be undone. If I'd had the power to give you a different father, I wouldn't hesitate. You deserve so much more."

I pulled my legs up onto the couch, tucking them to the side. "I know why you did what you did. I just don't know why you never told me."

Her fingers tapped lightly against the Christmas mug Gigi was so fond of. "At first you were too young and as time went by . . ." She shook her head. "I didn't want to blow up your world. As you grew older, I noticed little things that only another supernatural might see. Your powers were manifesting, and there was nothing I could do to stop them, no place I could hide you from who you are. I struggled for months over telling you, and it was Gigi who convinced me we needed to come home. I had every intention of telling you after you'd settled in, but you came into your powers quicker than I anticipated, and you adjusted so well. We made the right choice coming back here. In truth, I was scared. I didn't want you to hate me."

"I could never hate you, Mom. We're a team, you and I. Always have been. Always will be," I said, offering her a soft smile of encouragement. It was hard to see the female figure in my life vulnerable.

"He wasn't always so . . . ambitious," she finally decided, choosing her words carefully. "We started dating freshman year in high school, and it was a whirlwind romance. We were so in love and had dreams. Big dreams, but in hindsight, I should have seen it. He changed right before my eyes, but I was too blinded by my love for him. And then it was too late. I couldn't save him." Her eyes turned misty. "But maybe I could save you. So I ran. And kept running."

I was thankful for the warmth of the fire to relieve the chill that had settled into my veins. "What happened to him?" I asked.

She seemed to lose herself in the past before responding, her voice sad. "The temptation of darkness can be seductive, like a drug. Once you've had a taste, you crave more until it is all you can think about. It poisons the mind. Roth had a curious mind, like you, but he didn't have your strength. He would sneak across the borders of Havenwood Falls to experiment with his powers, which led him to some potent spells—dark magic. On more than one occasion, I followed him, fearful the Blackstone witch hunters would uncover his secret. He was a skilled warlock and learned quickly. By the time I realized he was no longer the boy I fell in love with, I was already pregnant with you, just a few months after graduation."

I sipped on my coffee as I listened. It was hard to believe this was a true story and not fantasy, but that could apply to most of my life. I'd heard of the Blackstone witch hunters from Beck, but only in passing.

"I desperately wanted that boy back and begged him to stop practicing," she continued. "He refused, breaking my heart, but I didn't have just myself to think about, so I ended things. I told Roth it was over. It was naive to think he would let me walk away. I was a possession to him. And I kept my pregnancy a secret; not even Gigi knew. The only people I confided in had been Mira and Ryle. The biggest mistake of my life."

Her coffee was forgotten, cold in her hand. I couldn't help but admire her poise and courage as she recounted what was the worst night of her life.

The sadness in her expression faded into worry. "Roth found out about you. I was only nine weeks pregnant and barely had time to contemplate the fact that I was going to be a mom. I don't know how your father discovered my secret, but if I had to guess, it was dark magic. He knew I was hiding something. Roth wasn't just curious; he was also extremely perceptive, especially when it came to me."

"You went to Mira and Ryle for help," I supplied.

She nodded, her finger circling around the rim of her cup. "I didn't know what else to do, who else to turn to, but I wish more than anything I had never sought their help. It seemed the only way, a simple spell to make Roth forget me. I refused to let him take you from me, which was exactly what he threatened."

God, my father sounded like such an asshat.

"I didn't know what he had planned that night. If I had, I would have tried to stop him. I would have warned Ryle and Mira. They were my best friends. I never would have let him hurt them."

It was clear Mom still tormented herself with the guilt of Ryle's death and her lost friendship with Mira. My heart squeezed for her.

"Styx gave me a vision of that night," I said softly.

Her eyes widened a fraction. "That doesn't surprise me. I haven't been back to the lake yet. I can't bring myself to go." She set aside the coffee and folded her hands in her lap. "He came upon us near Peacock Lake with a witch, Lyra Beaumont. She was in the middle of her spell, which had drained some of her energy, but even at full power, I don't think she would have been a match for Roth. He had grown stronger each day, and that night I feared him more than death itself." A shudder rolled through her petite frame as she relived that horrible event. "He struck with dark violence before we had a chance to defend ourselves. His target had been Lyra, to stop her from finishing the spell. Ryle threw himself in front of her. The spear of darkness hit him in the center of his chest. I'll never forget the look in his eyes, full of shock and pain."

A lump of emotion lodged itself in my throat.

"He killed him and just took off," I said, unable to disguise the repulsion in my voice.

Mom's voice faltered for an instant. "No. He might have done more harm, but that kind of magic doesn't go unnoticed in Havenwood Falls. It was a matter of minutes before Roth was surrounded. That night was the last time I saw him."

"He was sentenced to jail."

She nodded. "He was. Life without parole."

"Even with him locked away, you still decided to leave?"

"I didn't trust a supernatural prison would hold him, not even one bound by fae magic. Fear drove me from Havenwood Falls. I didn't want him anywhere near you. Gigi agreed. She helped me leave and find a safe place to stay until you were born. I made Gigi swear to never tell you. She gave me her word, but she didn't agree. I don't think his parents ever knew about you, but his family left Havenwood Falls shortly after his sentencing."

I couldn't imagine how alone she had felt. The picture was clearer but didn't make the burden I now faced any lighter. Did Mom know about the blood hex that had been passed down to me? If not, could I burden her with more guilt? I couldn't.

Maybe it was my turn to protect her.

# CHAPTER 9

The wind was howling and whipping outside the Academy building, the classroom of my Awakening Lab unusually cold. More than a week had passed since I'd found out about my father. I tucked my chin inside my hoodie and let the sleeves drape over my fingers. A shiver curled down my neck.

I glanced around the room. No one's teeth were chattering. No one else had goosebumps covering their skin. I seemed to be the only one freezing half to death.

My arms folded over my chest to keep the warmth close. Too bad Torent wasn't taking classes at the Academy. I could use a dose of his hellfire. The thought no sooner crossed my mind than I did feel something . . . something weird and unfamiliar. I glimpsed over my shoulder, my eyes darting over the class.

Again, I was alone in my suffering.

Not a single soul flinched as I did. Otis chewed on the end of his pen. He was a shifter with an infatuation for putting things in his mouth. Gianna continued to twirl her glossy hair around her finger, listening to her mom talk. The girl beside me snapped her gum.

But the eerie feeling continued shimmying up my spine until an odd tremor spread over my shoulders, down my arms, and into my fingertips. The first tendrils of unease bloomed in the pit of my belly like a vine of ivy twisting around my insides.

Returning my focus to Mrs. Augustine's lecture, I did my best to ignore the chill of concern that had taken up residence inside me. I couldn't shake the distinct feeling something was about to happen—something dark and unnatural. It was driving me crazy that no one else could sense it. Was I losing my mind?

*It's the fingers of death—my legacy.*

Unless Mrs. Augustine had suddenly become a dude with a deep voice, that had not been her speaking.

"I'm sorry. What did you say?" I blurted out before my brain caught up to my mouth.

Utter silence followed. Mrs. Augustine paused in her speech to address me. "Do you have a question, Mallory?"

I had a million questions, but I doubted everyone else in the class wanted to sit there as I peppered Mrs. Augustine with my inquiries about hexes, dead birds, and apparently now mysterious voices in my head. I shook my head. If I could have crawled under my desk and disappeared, I would have.

A few of the people around me shifted in their seats or chuckled. Amusing the class had not been my objective. My heart picked up its pace, and I could feel sweat dotting my palms. Any more outbursts like this, and I'd get kicked out of class.

Mrs. Augustine cleared her throat.

"Sorry, I, uh, didn't mean to interrupt." Maybe I was getting sick, not that I'd ever heard of the flu causing voices, but it could very well be a supernatural side effect. That was it. I had a supernatural flu bug. Gigi would definitely have a remedy for that.

*You're not sick, Mallory.*

Holy crap on a cracker. The voice burst my bubble.

Because there were still a few sets of eyes on me, I refrained from sticking my fingers in my ears to drown out the voice. I doubted it would help. Forcing myself to draw in several deep breaths, I attempted to curb the panic attack rising in my chest.

If I wasn't sick then it had to be stress. I needed sleep. Lots and lots of hard Z's.

*Nothing you do will stop death.*

Enough. My palms slammed on the desk, and I once again found the class staring at me. Heat painted my cheeks. "Sorry," I mouthed and returned to stare at the blank page of notebook paper in front of me.

*Death becomes you,* the voice hissed, causing a shiver to ripple through me.

That wasn't ominous.

Who was the voice? And what did they want with me? Did it have anything to do with the dead birds?

I didn't want death to become me. I didn't want this at all. None of it.

Gigi was out for the night, and Mom was watching TV on the couch when I got home after night class. Still shaken from what happened in Awakening Lab, I popped my head in to let her know I was home and headed upstairs to my room. Tonight was a bubble bath and a pound of chocolate kind of night.

My mind was already on the tub and the bath bomb I'd splurged on a few weeks ago as I walked through my bedroom door. I slipped my fingers under my hoodie and whipped it off. Tossing it aside, I unbuttoned my jeans and found a pair of sparkling eyes staring at me from the corner of my room.

I yelped, equal parts fear and shock coursing through me.

*Holy fuck.*

Someone was sitting in my room—in the dark—like a total serial killer. My powers instinctually activated, going into defense mode. I didn't know what this dark figure wanted, but if he had come to kill me, he was going to have a fight on his hands. My brain automatically assumed it was a guy, but my stalker could very well have been female. It was hard to tell in the dark.

*No way that's Brooklyn. Is it?*

If anyone suffered from an obsession with me, my money was on my nymph nemesis. I'd hate to say that ten times fast.

Throwing out my hand, I summoned the closest metal object I could find in my room—a nail file from my desk—and sent it sailing toward the mysterious perp with glowing violet eyes.

Wait.

*Is that flecks of gold I see in them?*

There was only one person with eyes like that.

"Torent?" my voice squeaked in the dark. At the last second, I stopped the nail file flying across my room just short of gouging Torent's eyeball.

"Do you think you can drop the pointy object before you accidentally scar my handsome face?" The texture of his voice was silky as night and wicked.

A whoosh of air left my lungs, and I set the nail file on the dresser. "It would serve you right for scaring the shit out of me. How did you get in here?"

He stood up, and a beam of moonlight streaked over the left side of his cheek. I caught a hint of a smirk on his lips. "Haven't you learned? Locks can't keep me out."

Shutting the door to the hallway, I pressed my back into it.

"Okay. That still doesn't explain why you snuck into my bedroom," I hissed, attempting to keep my voice low so as not to alert Mom anything was amiss. I had a boy in my room. Not just any boy. A hot demon I couldn't seem to keep my hands off.

This was bad. Like epically bad.

A muscle feathered in his cheek. "You didn't answer my text, and I got worried, so I came to check on you."

Damn demon. "You almost lost an eyeball."

He lifted a brow, eyeing the nail file on the dresser. "I noticed."

"As you can see, I'm fine. You should leave." *Quick, before I do something reckless like kiss you.*

His long legs easily crossed the room, and the smell that was uniquely Torent reached my nose. *Why does he have to smell so good?*

"Do you have a problem with being in the same room as me?" he asked.

Uh, I could barely breathe the same air as him without wanting to tackle him and kiss him to death.

"Torent, you shouldn't be here. It's dangerous to be near me. If anything happened to you . . ." My voice trailed off, emotion clogging my throat.

I blinked, and he was suddenly in front of me. "I might not be immortal, but demons don't die easily."

Now that he was here, I wanted him to stay more than I wanted that bubble bath. I chewed on the inside of my lip, wrestling with myself. What happened in class tonight came back to haunt me. Death. The stench of it lingered on me like cigarette smoke. One of the reasons I had craved a bath. I wanted to rid myself of the dirty feeling it left stained on my skin.

Torent's finger slipped under my chin, and he peered into my eyes. It was as if he could reach my soul. "What happened?" he demanded.

A smart guy would have already run far away from me, but not Torent. He headed straight for the heart of danger and would face the greatest of evils to protect those he cared about. I was one of those people. My whole body radiated like the center of a star, casting points of light to every finger and toe.

Overwhelmed with an outpouring of emotion that strongly resembled love, I opened my mouth to tell him—

Then my bedroom window shattered.

Glass sprayed all over the room, and a streak of black sliced through the air. Torent's reflexes kicked in, tucking me against his body as he dropped down to the ground, shielding me from the raining glass. The sound was ear piercing, causing my whole body to wince. When the dust settled, a large mangled crow lay on my floor, covered in a pool of glass fragments.

God damn. How many birds was this curse going to kill before I figured out how to break it? There was no way I was going to let what my father did take me down too. I would find a way to end this torment.

"Mallory!" My name belted from downstairs, followed by rapid footsteps. My mom was coming, and we were less than a minute away from being busted.

Lifting my head, I met Torent's luminous gaze. "Hide," I ordered him, pushing at his chest.

He didn't immediately move, to my frustration. "You owe me a thanks, crash car."

"I'll give you a million thanks, just get in the closet." His grin was going to make me regret those words, but he disappeared into the shadows just as my bedroom door whipped open.

I carefully got to my feet and brushed the glass off me. Argh. It was in my hair. Torent was sliding the closet door softly closed.

Mom stood in the threshold, her eyes sweeping over the disarray of my room with horror before finding me. "What happened? Oh, my God. Are you hurt?"

She rushed over, running her fingers over my face looking for cuts.

"I'm fine," I assured softly.

Her eyes once again roamed over the catastrophe that was my room, landing on the dead bird. It was simple math to put two and two together.

"Did he fly through your window?" she asked, incredulity lacing her tone.

"I was about to take a bath, and he came crashing through the window. I didn't know birds had that kind of strength."

Her lips pinched together. "They don't normally." Relaxing her features, she rubbed her hands up and down my arms to comfort me . . . or herself. I wasn't sure which. "The important thing is you're okay. I'll help you clean up the glass and secure the window until we can call someone tomorrow to fix it."

I nodded, feeling numb. The curse was progressing, and I didn't know what to do about it.

"Are you sure you're okay?" she asked, noticing the odd expression that had crept onto my face.

I couldn't very well tell her Torent had shielded me. Doing everything in my power to not look at the closet, I replied, "I'm still a bit shaken up."

She nodded and left to grab supplies. A cold gust of wind hurtled through what was left of the jagged window. I turned to the closet, spotting the glowing violet eyes.

"Don't move," I told him. "And don't think about going through my stuff."

A husky chuckle came through the crack as if he had been caught red-handed. I should have shoved him out the broken window before Mom came back, but I didn't want him to leave, so in the closet he stayed.

I swept up the pieces of glass. Mom disposed of the bird, wrinkling her nose in the process and both of us trying to not squeal like little girls. Knowing Torent, it was either torture or entertaining watching Mom and me handle the cleanup. It was probably grating on his hero soul to be unable to swoop in and save the day. That was what he was good at.

Together we covered the window with plastic and sealed it up with tape. It wasn't pretty but would do for the night. Mom brought up a space heater from the basement to make sure I didn't freeze to death. I was grateful Gigi was out tonight with her "bridge club"—a cover for the little old ladies of Havenwood Falls to get together and gossip.

The door clicked shut behind Mom twenty minutes later, and I spun around. Torent emerged from the closet dressed in all black. He had ditched his hoodie, leaving the cotton T-shirt stretching across his chest. I was relieved he hadn't come out with a thong on his head. It was mortifying enough knowing he had been eavesdropping on Mom and me.

My eyes darted over his face like a mermaid yearning for the sea, but it was the sight of something red on the side of his neck that had me crossing to him.

"You're bleeding," I whispered, lifting to inspect the damage. It was only a nick, most of the blood dried.

He hissed through his teeth, reaching for my hand. "Don't poke at it."

My lips twitched, and I tried to hide my amusement. "Sorry."

Encircling my wrist, he brought my hand to his chest, covering it with one of his own. "The curse is escalating."

*Tell me something I don't know.* My grin slipped off my face. "All the more reason for you to not be here. You should keep your distance."

He walked over to my bed and fluffed a pillow, then dropped down on top of it, making himself comfortable. The mattress bounced under his weight. "Not going to happen. I plan on sticking close just in case anything else weird happens."

"By close, you mean you're planning on spending the night? In my room? With me?" *Way to not sound lame, Mallory.*

He grinned and patted the bed.

This was insane, and yet I was calmer. I should be freaking the eff out, but having Torent near made me worry a little less.

"What are you doing?" I inquired, though it was crystal clear what he was up to.

Sprawled on his back, he laced his fingers under his head in a sign he had no intention of leaving. "What does it look like?"

I stood in the center of the room like a lost puppy. "Like you're taking up more than half of my bed."

What did he expect? For me to climb in beside him?

Those lips formed a grin. "Isn't it past your bedtime? You've had kind of a rough day."

"Is that so?" How could any single guy look so good lying in a soft pink bed?

Long lashes framed his eyes, drawing my attention to his face. "Mallory, come here."

A shiver skipped over my skin.

"I need to use the bathroom," I announced, feeling my cheeks brighten in color. *Smooth, Mal.* I turned and hightailed it to the safety of my adjoining bathroom to shower, change, and brush my teeth. Close quarters with Torent called for fresh breath, and I doubted he would appreciate the glass in my hair. Not that I was anticipating anything to happen between us, but I was a girl who liked to be prepared for all possibilities.

Again I found myself fidgeting and staring at the floor. What was wrong with me? I stood in the doorway, telling myself I had nothing to be nervous about. This was just Torent.

His eyes glided over me in an unhurried perusal. "I'm not going to attack you like an animal."

My heart tripped up in my chest as my feet padded slowly over the floor. Was I seriously getting in bed with a demon? I climbed in, keeping my gaze glued to his, and rested my cheek on the pillow. I turned on my side.

"You don't need to stay. I'm fine," I insisted, but I really did want him to stay for purely selfish reasons.

"I'm staying. I don't want any more surprises."

That made two of us. I'd met my quota for the day. My heart couldn't take more. Then again, I wasn't sure my heart could take sleeping alongside Torent Stark. Sex and all things naughty should have been the furthest thing from my mind, but he smelled so good.

Torent mistook my nervousness. "We're going to figure out how to defeat this curse."

"I don't know where to start. What if I end up like him?" I glanced away, staring at where our feet lay at the end of the bed.

His knuckles brushed along my cheek, drawing my eyes back to him. "Our parents don't define us, crash car. We make our own fate. We're all capable of darkness, but that doesn't mean we're evil. You're many things, but malicious is not one of them. Don't doubt who you are."

That was the thing. I didn't know who I was anymore.

# CHAPTER 10

"*I* don't want to talk about the curse anymore. Tell me about your family. I want to know more about what it's like being a demon." A distraction was what I needed, and Torent provided the perfect outlet to get my mind off the curse.

He opened an arm. "Get comfortable, crash car. This is going to take all night."

"Perfect," I replied dryly, but curled up against him, laying my damp head in the nook of his arm. Sleep was out of reach for me tonight. The splintering of glass still echoed in my ears.

His fingers slipped over my hand relaxing on his chest. "If you want a distraction . . ." The suggestion in his voice made my belly flutter. It was as if he could read my mind.

I lifted my head slightly to peer down at him with a ghost of a smile on my lips. "As tempting as it is, and believe me I'm seriously tempted, it's not a good idea. I don't trust myself."

Shifting his head on the pillow, he kept our fingers laced together. Seconds later, my ceiling was painted with pink, purple, and teal sparkling lights dancing. "I'm here to protect you, not the other way around."

"And why can't I be the hero for once?" I asked blandly.

"Because I'm not the one with a death curse."

I nudged him in the side. "Hey. I thought we weren't going to talk about the curse."

"Right," he agreed, turning his gaze upward to watch the colors frolic and twinkle. "Well, my family is insane, volatile, treacherous, and amazing," he added, grinning. I could hear how much he cared for them. "And those are just my brothers."

"What about your parents?" I inquired, curious about the people who had created such a perfect male. I pressed my chin on his chest so I could stare at his face. Splashes of colored light reflected over his skin.

"My father is larger than life with a laugh that booms across a crowded room. And my mom is petite, but don't let her size fool you. She isn't a woman to mess with."

"I can't wait to meet your family," I said, sort of kidding.

He laughed. "They are going to love you."

A pack of menacing demons . . . I wondered what they would think of their youngest son dating a nymph.

"Do you always pursue girls this hard?" I asked the question that had been on my mind for weeks.

His eyes deepened in color. "Never."

I believed him. "Then why me?"

"Does there need to be a reason?" he countered.

He wasn't getting out of it that easily. I sincerely wanted to know what it was that made me different from every other girl. I wasn't special or prettier. I was just me, and I was curious how *he* saw me. I gave him a pointed look, the lines in my face set.

His leaned forward so our noses were only inches apart. "You're more beautiful than any enchanted meadow. You're stubborn but filled with goodness. You care more about other people than yourself. And no one has ever made me feel the way I do when we're together."

Sweet hell. His words caused a chain reaction to go off inside me as if my veins were filled with millions of starlights. How did I respond to an admission like that? Thank you didn't seem to cut it.

"You're nothing like I first thought." He was so much more.

"And what exactly was your first impression of me, other than I was extraordinarily good looking?"

I snorted. "You just proved my initial thought—that you were arrogant." But I had been wrong.

We talked for hours until I was barely able to keep my eyes open and the day was finally catching up to me. I dozed off. It was a miracle, considering I'd spent a creepy amount of time staring at Torent while he slept. He looked nothing like a demon and everything like an angel.

I was on the edge of consciousness, but not fully ready to give up sleep. My body was burning like the sun, and I couldn't figure out why. Did I have a fever? Had someone cranked the heat? No. It wasn't that kind of heat, not the sweat-drenching-over-my-skin-heat.

This was internal and made me tremble. With shallow, uneven breaths, my eyes fluttered open, and I tilted my head to the side, leaning into the dreamy sensation. It was only then I realized it was Torent's lips causing my hormones to go haywire.

His mouth was restless, rushing down my neck and over a bare shoulder. The T-shirt I had worn to bed had slipped off to the side, giving him all the access he desired. It was as if it was vital for him to taste all of me. My brain foggy from the sudden onslaught of sensations rocking through my body, I couldn't tell if this was a dream or very real.

I wanted it to be real.

"Mallory," my name tumbled from his lips, low and vibrant like an enchanting prayer. I felt worshiped. "Mallory?" he whispered again, but this time in question—he was asking permission.

I didn't know whose mouth found whose, but our lips met. The kiss started out sweet and exploratory, but it didn't stay that way for long. As he took my mouth deeper, our tongues twined, the cool metal of his piercing teasing me. It only took that one kiss for me to make a decision. I wanted this. I wanted Torent.

*What about the hex?* a voice echoed in my head. The blood hex would continue weaving itself in my veins, growing stronger, to the point it might progress from plants and birds to those I cared about.

For the briefest of moments, I pulled away. Was I making a mistake?

Every pore in my body was aware of Torent. His mouth reclaimed mine, and I was no longer thinking at all. Power soared inside me, the fire spreading fast and wildly.

His hands dove into my hair, fingers raking desperately to pull me closer.

"Tell me this is okay?" he murmured gruffly. "I'll stop if this isn't what you want." The idea sounded as if it pained him, but I knew from the bottom of my heart it would only take one word from me and he would stop.

I swallowed, letting my hands frame either side of his face. "I want this. I want you," I whispered, brushing my lips across his.

His entire body relaxed into mine, and I paused to shed my shirt. He watched my every move, hardly breathing. A ravenous, primal hunger darkened his eyes that were more gold than violet. I should have been afraid or at the very least cautious, but I felt neither.

Gentle hands explored my body, and I tried not to let my insecurities get in the way.

"You're so beautiful," he said, tracing lazy patterns over my belly.

I trembled at his touch.

"Are you scared?" he asked, gazing into my eyes.

I'd never seen such a color before, the way his human and demon eyes blended together. I was awestruck by him. "No. I'm not afraid. Not of you. Maybe a little of how you make me feel."

His head angled to the side, regarding me with a devastating smile. "How do I make you feel?"

Every fiber in my body was screaming for me to tell him that I loved him. Instead, I showed him. Fisting my fingers into his silky hair, I ground my lips to his, yielding completely to the storm swirling inside me. Everything beyond this room, beyond Torent, became a void of darkness.

My bare legs hooked behind his, and I ran my ankle down his muscular calf. He breathed my name over and over again. I couldn't tell where I ended and he began. He was mine, and I was his. Our bodies were meant to be together; I didn't know how else to describe it. The connection between us was like fire, burning and intense. We clung to one another, body to body, as the shimmer of pleasure glistened over our skin. The only sound in the room was the beating of our hearts in perfect wild harmony.

Afterward, I lay in his arms, our legs intertwined, and I told him I loved him . . . in my head.

The next time I woke up, beams of warm sunlight were taking their first peek over the horizon as the last dusting of stars winked out of the sky. Utter calmness seemed to settle over the world.

I stretched out in bed, my heart bursting with happiness and so many other emotions. Why did it feel like this demon belonged in my bed—at my side?

I didn't want to start the day. In fact, I wanted to stay here with Torent, but I doubted Mom or Gigi would agree. They would be getting up soon, and it would be wise if Torent was gone before then, but looking at him sleeping peacefully beside me, I didn't have the heart to disturb him. Plus, he was mesmerizing to stare at.

I should really stop, but I couldn't help myself.

Lifting a hand, I brushed a stray strand of hair off the side of his face and watched his lips slowly begin to curve.

"Good morning," he said huskily, his eyes still closed.

My mouth echoed his grin. "Hey."

This didn't need to be awkward, so I told myself to be cool, and *hey* was what I'd come up with. Real cool.

Those long legs stretched like a predator cat's after a long night's nap. "How did you sleep?"

My cheek pressed into the top of my hands as I turned on my side. "I survived the night, and my window's still broken."

His lips curled. "My job here is done."

And I didn't kill him while he slept—that was something. Perhaps the hex was only effective on animals and plants?

I loved my wishful thinking, but it gave me something to cling to—hope.

"Mallory!" Mom shouted my name from down the hall. "You're going to be late for school."

Shit. I'd completely forgotten it was a weekday. There would be no lazy morning snuggles.

I bolted upright on the bed, my sudden wide eyes bouncing from the closed door to Torent. His dark messy hair was spread out over the white pillow. He didn't so much as flinch at the sound of my Mom's voice.

"What are you doing?" I shrieked in a hushed whisper. "You've got to go. Now!" I said, pushing at his heavy body.

Why did he have so many muscles? It made shoving him off the bed nearly impossible.

Sitting up, he ran his hand through his hair. "You look cute frazzled."

Oh, my God. He was still naked. I was naked! I jumped out of bed, throwing on a shirt and locating his discarded shirt and jeans.

"Quick, get dressed," I ordered, throwing the clothes at him. The shirt landed on his face. I wasted no time crossing back to the bed. My fingers latched on to his arm, and I yanked.

With an oomph, Torent tumbled to the floor.

"Mallory, are you okay?" Mom's voice carried through from the other side of the door.

"Yes, just getting dressed," I hollered back, buying myself a few minutes.

Torent looked up at me from the floor. "You're lucky I don't pull you down here with me."

I blew at the disarray of hair that had fallen into my face. "Now is not the time for games, Stark. And why aren't your clothes on yet?"

His smile was troublesome. "Is my nakedness bothering you?"

"Yes! And unless you want my mom to string you up by your balls, you need to move your fine ass."

The grin on his lips did not waver. He was not in the least intimidated by my threat. "It is a pretty spectacular ass."

"Torent," I groaned, and it was enough to get him moving. As he finally dressed, I scanned the room and realized I had a problem. Panic tore inside me. "How the hell did you get in here?" I asked, realizing I needed a way to get him out of my room undetected.

"Through the window," he answered, blasé.

Both our heads whipped toward the broken and taped up glass.

"Shit," I mumbled under my breath. "That isn't going to work now." My fingers dashed through my hair as I racked my brain for a plan.

His pants were on now but unbuttoned as he slipped his T-shirt over his head. "Don't panic. We'll figure something out."

Too late.

My pulse had already quickened, my chest tightening. "You'd better hurry and come up with a stellar idea, because I've got nothing."

A light rap of knuckles sounded on my door. "Honey? Gigi wants to know if Torent wants breakfast."

My face fell. *Damn. Damn. Damn.* Living with a bunch of magical nymphs was going to be hell on my dating life . . . now that I had one. There was no going back after last night.

The notorious demon's lips twitched. "I would love breakfast," he mouthed.

I elbowed him in the gut and went to the door, throwing it open. I tried to angle my body in such a way that Torent's form was obscured.

"I can explain." The words popped out of my mouth.

Mom stood on the other side of the door attempting to school her expression, but I caught the sparkle of amusement in her eyes.

Her perfect daughter getting caught with a boy in her room. I wouldn't be surprised if she was a bit proud too.

"You think you're the first person to sneak a boy into this house? I've got a tip for you. Nothing gets past Gigi's eyes. I learned that the hard way." She tweaked the end of my nose. "Morning, Torent," she said, her gaze going past me into my bedroom, where Torent was standing with his hands shoved into his jeans.

Those vibrant violet eyes glinted with humor. "Good morning, Ms. Whitt."

"Didn't I tell you to call me Wendy?" She wrinkled her nose. "Ms. Whitt makes me sound old." And Mom definitely didn't want to be that.

"He was just leaving," I interjected before things could possibly get any weirder.

"Uh-huh," Mom said, pursing her lips. "Just don't be late for school again, okay?" She turned and strutted down the hall, her hips swinging from side to side.

I shut the door and leaned my back against it. *Why does this stuff happen to me?* I wanted nothing more than to climb under my bed and never leave my room again, let alone have to face Gigi.

Torent, seeing the distraught expression on my face, laughed. "This has been the most fun I've had in a while. You're something else."

The features on my face remained impassive. "Not funny."

"It kind of is."

"Oh, yeah?" I grabbed the closest thing I could find and chucked it at his head. He caught the fuzzy slipper midair, laughing harder. "You're the one who is going to be doing the walk of shame into class this morning," I snapped, thinking stupidly that would wipe the smirk off his lips.

The joke was on me.

"It was worth it," he said, his deep tone sexy as sin.

My heart cartwheeled.

# CHAPTER 11

*T*orent had returned my car last week good as new. You'd never be able to tell the windshield had been shattered. We drove separately to school, and I told myself some space was a good thing, especially after the embarrassing morning. My cheeks had never been so red when I shuffled downstairs, ushering Torent out. Gigi didn't say a word, but I didn't doubt I would get one of her talks after school.

Not that I minded them. Truthfully, most of Gigi's advice was spot on. My family might be eccentric, but living with all women had taught me how to be strong and independent.

At lunch, Beck and I drove over to Sakura Buffet to grab something to eat. It was close to school, and the service was quick. We didn't always leave campus for lunch, but today I needed to get out of the stuffy classrooms for a bit, and my sudden craving for Chinese food was too mighty to ignore.

A little bell rang over the door as we walked over the threshold and into the dining room. We went up to the buffet bar. The cashier rang up our orders and handed us two plates. Beck and I moseyed down the line, filling our plates with sweet and sour chicken, rice, noodles, egg rolls, and some kind of beef.

Spotting an empty booth that overlooked the parking lot, we slid in and set our plates down.

"God, I'm starving," I said, picking up my fork.

"Maybe it might have something to do with your late nights with Torent?" Beck prodded. "Have you taken my advice?"

He was convinced having sex with Torent would loosen me up. I hated to admit he might have been right.

Something in my expression must have triggered his internal sex alarm. "Oh. My. God. You did it, didn't you? You actually took my advice."

Twirling my fork in the soft noodles, I did everything I could to keep a straight face, including shoving the fork into my mouth.

"I don't know what you're talking about," I mumbled, in what sounded like one long word.

He picked up his egg roll and dunked it into some sweet and sour sauce.

"Then why am I still detecting tension in your aura?" he countered, calling my bullshit.

Damn wolf senses. Time for a quick topic change before half the restaurant got intimate details about my love life.

"We have important things to discuss," I said, leaning over the table and dropping my voice.

He waved his egg roll in the air. "What could possibly be more important than what Torent can do in the bedroom?"

I rolled my eyes, but a hint of a smile curved my lips. The memories were too incredible to suppress. I shook my head. *Focus, Mal. And not on Torent's body.* "I need to break a hex. What do you got?"

A scoop of rice that was halfway to his mouth fell off his fork. "You figured out it's a hex?"

The door jingled behind us, and a group of kids from our school sauntered in, including Brooklyn and her nymph cronies.

"Shhh. I'd rather not have the whole school talking about me . . . more than they already are," I added at the lift of Beck's brow.

He stabbed a piece of chicken with the end of his fork. "We need code words for this shit, considering it keeps coming up."

Talking about the supernatural world out in the open was forbidden. Humans might overhear.

"I'm open to suggestions, but I really need your help."

"Beck to the rescue. What kind of . . . uh, cake are we talking about?"

"Cake?" I echoed. "That's the word you chose?"

His shoulders lifted up in a lazy shrug. "I'm eating. What did you expect? It was the first thing that popped into my head."

"It's the kind of cake that kills animals and plants. A death cake," I whispered.

His silver eyes went wide. "Jesus, Mal. You sleep with a demon, and he serves you cake afterward? I never would have pegged Torent as that kind of guy."

I rolled my eyes. "He isn't. The cake has nothing to do with him. It's my father who baked the cake and burned it."

This whole food analogy was absurd. Next time I had something secret and important to discuss with Beck, it was not going to be in a public place. Some lessons about being a supernatural were harder to implement into my daily life.

He swallowed, trying to control the shock on his face and not choke at the same time. "Your father?"

I nodded. "I dug up some dirt on him after I went to Peacock Lake with Torent. Remember the whole milkshake incident?"

"How could I forget? It's going to go down in HFH history as one of the greatest moments ever."

Suppressing another series of eye rolls, I continued to tell him what I'd learned about my father and Brooklyn's family without actually referring to anything supernatural. I then told him about the window last night and why Torent had spent the night but left out the *other* details. The last thing I needed was Beck to go off on another sex tangent.

"So I need to figure out how to throw out the cake before it poisons someone I love." Or destroys me.

"Got it. When it comes to investigation, I'm your guy." I could already see the wheels spinning in his head. Research and snooping were Beck's specialty. He was the nerdy king, in a really cool way.

"That's what I was counting on." If anyone could find something about a death curse, it was Beck.

"How much time do we have before things go boom?" he inquired.

Boom? I sure as hell hoped things didn't explode. "I'm not sure. It seems to be progressing though."

"Let's rendezvous after school. I know someone who might be able to help. Have you mentioned anything to your mom?"

I crossed my legs under the table. "Not about the cake. We talked about my father and what happened that night, but she's already carrying so much guilt. I'd rather not involve her unless I have to."

Beck raised his brows. "And Torent?"

Shoving the rice around on my plate, dread wormed its way into the bottom of my belly, making the food I'd eaten roll. "He's already involved."

Beck gave me one of his shithead grins. "I knew it. You loooove him."

I flung a pea at him. "Say that again and I'll bend that fork around your neck."

His grin only grew.

What the hell were friends for if not to help you when shit was about to hit the fan? Having a shifter nerd for a best friend was handy. It was as if the universe knew I would need someone like him when I moved to Havenwood Falls to keep me out of danger.

"I want to hear more about what happened last night, and not the window thing—the stuff after that." Beck waggled his brows.

School had ended, and the two of us were in my car, driving to someone's house. He had given me directions and instructed me to drive. Like the good little sheep I was, I followed. I didn't have any other options. If I didn't need to keep both hands on the wheel or risk going off the road, I would have whacked him on the back of the head.

"I'm a walking death time bomb, and you want to talk about my sex life?"

He looked at me without blinking. "Duh. How else am I going to live vicariously through you?"

"Where are we going?" I asked again, attempting to divert the conversation for the fifth time since school ended.

He glanced sideways at me. "I know what you're doing."

I smiled at him and batted my eyes. Of course he did. I'd been avoiding his attempts all day to get me to dish the deets on my night with Torent. Some things were meant to stay private.

"She's a witch." That was all the information he revealed. Just who was this mysterious witch?

It made sense to seek out another witch's help to break a hex. "And you think she can break the curse?"

"That's the thing about curses. They're tricky. It depends on the type of curse and the magic the witch used to cast it. If she can't break it, then maybe she can at least help us search for a way."

It was hard to not get my hopes up, but if this didn't shed some light on my situation, I was going to have to involve my mom, and that was the last thing I wanted to do.

We pulled up to a gated community, and my car idled in the cold, the exhaust billowing white smoke behind us as we waited to be let through. Iron fences bordered the upscale neighborhood of Havenwood Heights. My fingers tapped on the steering wheel with nerves and impatience.

"Does she know we're coming?"

"She knows," Beck assured with a ghost of a smirk on his lips. "Just wait for it."

*What for what?*

And then it happened. There was no gate keeper, no one to wave us through, but the beautifully designed gate suddenly, slowly swung open like magic.

It wasn't *like* magic. It was magic. The tang of it scented the air.

"She knows we're here," Beck announced, looking smug.

"Wonderful," I mumbled, wondering what kind of witch we were seeing—light or dark? I probably should have asked Beck before I agreed to go up here, but I trusted him. If he believed she could help, then what was the harm in talking to her, regardless of which side of the field she waved her wand for?

*Your father chose dark magic and look where that got him,* a little voice in my head reminded me.

In prison.

I made a decision right there. If breaking the hex required the use of dark magic, then I had to find another way. My soul was a sacrifice I wasn't willing to make. No one I cared about would be hurt by this darkness. It stopped with me.

I guided my car through the gates as my eyes absorbed the enormous old houses. Aspens and evergreen trees separated each estate. Many of the homes had a Gothic style I found interesting. Any other time, I would have loved to drive around and gawk at the craftsmanship.

"The founding families of the town live here," Beck told me, seeing my eyes linger over the houses as we passed by. "Lots of old money."

I blinked. "Old or new, I'd take any money. I'm not picky."

"Same," Beck agreed, smiling. The road wound as we drove deeper into the community of Havenwood Heights. "Turn left here," he advised when I came up to a fork in the road.

"It's so quiet here. I can't decide if it's eerie or peaceful."

Beck's eyes sharpened. "I'd say it's both. A lot of power and magic dwell here."

A shudder rolled through me. "I'll say so."

"That's her house there." He pointed to the right side of the street where it curved into a cul-de-sac.

I pulled my car up to the side of the road outside a three-story mansion. The exterior was a deep brownish-red brick with white trim that popped against the dark walls. Ivy clung and climbed over the arched windows. Two round towers flanked the house on both sides. A set of double doors greeted us as we strutted up the stone pathway from the driveway.

"How do you know her again?"

"School, but we don't talk much outside of class. Different social circles."

"Can we trust her not to blab to the entire school?" I inquired.

"She's trustworthy," he assured.

I exhaled and extended my hand to press the doorbell, but my finger never reached the glowing button. One of the massive doors swung open, and a woman in her forties with long dark curly hair swept into a messy bun stood in the doorway.

"Hello, Mallory. Beck." She nodded at my best friend beside me.

My mouth dropped open as I continued to stare at Ronya Augustine, my Awakening Lab teacher.

"You're the witch?" I blurted.

# CHAPTER 12

She winked, her eyes sparkling. "Life is just full of surprises, isn't it?"

I'll freakin' say.

Gesturing with a sweeping motion of her hand, she stepped to the side. "Come in. Beck mentioned you might be in need of some help."

I cleared my throat. "Yes, thank you," I replied, hoping the stunned expression would soon leave my face. As we followed Mrs. Augustine down her hallway, I nudged Beck in the side. "Why didn't you tell me your witch was a teacher?" I whispered between my teeth.

"You know the rules," he gritted back.

Humans couldn't know we existed, and talking about supernaturals in public was highly frowned upon due to rule number one.

Beck and I sat on a plush cranberry-colored couch decorated in a paisley pattern. It was one of the softest pieces of furniture I'd ever sat on. A fire was burning low embers in the hearth, filling the expansive ceilings with the sounds of crackling wood. The room oozed warmth.

In my head, I pictured a black cauldron with murky green goop bubbling over a fire and a broomstick leaning against the wall. Nothing could have been further from the reality of Mrs. Augustine's home. It was absolutely lovely.

"Tell me why you think you need my talents?" she asked, getting straight to the point. I appreciated her directness.

"Mallory is hexed," Beck proclaimed candidly.

Mrs. Augustine's eyes bounced between us, brows lifting ever so slightly. "I see. Tell me why you think you're cursed, Mallory," she directed at me.

Under these conditions, I figured it was best to hold nothing back. "Goddess Styx told me that a blood hex was inflicted on my father, and I inherited his blood debt when I came into my gifts, being his only child."

Her expression remained unmoved, and I took that as a good sign. "Do you know what kind of blood hex we're dealing with?"

I paused, unable to answer immediately. It was difficult to admit what I was afflicted with. "Death," I said flatly.

The room went utterly silent. I swear even the fire in the hearth stopped breathing for a moment. Mrs. Augustine took a deep sigh. "A blood spell is serious magic. Do you know who cast the spell?"

I shook my head. "No, not exactly."

Her lips pursed together. "Well, it would be helpful if we knew more about the curse and its origin, but considering who your father was, we'll have to work with what we got."

"You can help me?" I tried to keep the desperate hope at bay, but this was my only hope.

"I'm going to do my best. This is a kind of curse that doesn't have room for error, or you can accelerate its potency."

"We definitely don't want to do that," Beck said, echoing my thoughts.

Mrs. Augustine uncrossed her legs and stood up before going to a bookshelf on the same wall as the fireplace. Her fingers ran along the spines, searching for a specific book. They all looked old and dusty to me.

"Here it is," she said, tapping her finger on the spine before removing it from the shelf. She didn't immediately come back to the chair but stroked her hand down the front of the cover as if she was paying homage to the words that lay between the pages. "This has been in the Vanden family—my family—for generations." Her feet sank into the plush carpet as she came to sit back down with the book resting in her lap.

I got my first look at the spellbook I prayed would rid me of this hex. The leather bounds were weathered and frayed slightly, as if the book had been quite loved. The cover had an emblem on it, possibly the Vanden Coven's crest. It was a piece of history, and I wanted to touch it, was drawn to it. The book itself seemed to pulse with energy that woke up the nymph inside me.

I wasn't the only one who felt it.

"Holy shit," Beck exhaled, drawing my gaze to the shifter at my left. His eyes were burning like hot molten silver, hands clenching the end of the couch cushion.

I wanted to ask him if he was okay but thought it might be better not to draw attention to the pull of what we all felt, so I refocused my attention onto the book.

Mrs. Augustine had opened it up and was flipping through the pages until she came about midway through. Her finger skimmed over the text. "Hmm. That's what I thought." She adjusted her glasses and glanced upward at Beck and me. "A blood spell requires blood to break it."

"I hope you're not squeamish," Beck commented.

I shot him a droll look, because I was exactly that when it came to blood . . . and needles . . . and sacred knives used in magic.

"What does that mean? I need to sacrifice some of my own blood?" I asked.

"Or get a vampire to siphon it," Beck mumbled. He was so not helping.

A light shone in Mrs. Augustine's eyes. "You'll need more than your blood. This kind of spell is created with darkness. It must be broken with both light and dark. The blood of a goddess is as pure as it comes."

It was the dark that had me worried. That was exactly what had started this mess.

"And the dark?" I inquired.

"Demon blood," Beck piped in.

I turned to Mrs. Augustine for confirmation. She mulled it over for a hot minute. "Yes. A demon would do."

"But not all demons are bad," I opposed, making sure I had all my supernatural facts correct.

"No, but the root of their heritage is, just as the origin of yours is good," she explained.

Beck crossed his legs and leaned back into the feather soft cushions. "How lucky for you that you're dating a demon. Makes things less complicated."

I frowned at Beck. "How so?"

"You don't have to go hunting one down now," Beck said.

"Torent is only half demon," I pointed out.

Mrs. Augustine took the floor again. "Many of us have blood that's been diluted down through the ages, but the essence of where we come from is still there. I don't think the spell requires purity. A demon's blood, combined with yours, should be strong enough to weaken the touch of death."

I pushed against the unease that had slithered inside me. This was what I had asked for—a way to rid myself of the death following me. "Great. Now I have to convince him to give me his blood."

Beck's lip gave a one-sided shrug. "Shouldn't be hard. He's in love with you, after all."

I elbowed Beck in the side.

"What do I do with the blood?" I inquired to Mrs. Augustine. Details were important when dealing with magic. "Spread on the ground in a star or something during a full moon?"

Mrs. Augustine continued to read through the old text. When she lifted her gaze, unease skittered through me. Something in her eyes alarmed me. "You drink it."

That's what I was afraid of. "Wonderful. I'm a bloodsucker now. I can't drink his blood."

"You will if you want to stop randomly killing things," Beck snapped.

He had a point. I did want the curse to stop. "Am I supposed to walk up to him and ask to suck his blood? That's not creepy or anything."

Beck rubbed the tip of his nose. "Like you said. Vamps do it all the time. Not a big deal. Put it in a milkshake."

I wrinkled my nose. "Except I'm not a vamp. I'm a water nymph. No blood."

Beck brushed off my abhorrence to blood with a noise in the back of his throat. "He'll probably be all into it. Make it sexy or something. Suck on his neck," he offered.

"You're so not helping," I groaned, dropping my face into my hands.

"Hey, I did find someone to help you break the curse, didn't I?" he reminded me. What a good friend he was.

I lifted my chin. "Yes, and I love you for it. I seriously don't know what I would do without you."

Beck's eyes twinkled. "I could only imagine the walking hot mess you'd be."

"Before anyone goes drinking someone's blood," Mrs. Augustine interrupted. She had the patience of a saint, listening to Beck and I ramble without telling either of us to chill out. One of the reasons she was a great teacher. "You need to bring me the blood so I can enchant it first, and it can't be done just anywhere. We'll need to return to the spot where your father last cast his magic."

There was always a catch.

I swallowed. The idea of returning to the place where a boy had been killed and my life had been altered before I was born gave me chills. "And this will end the hex?"

"Yes, I believe so," Mrs. Augustine said, giving me a soft smile. "A full moon would give the spell its most potency."

In theory, it sounded too simple. I found that the simplest things were often those hardest to achieve, so I was under no delusion that ridding myself of death would be easy.

Beck and I left Mrs. Augustine with a solution, but I didn't feel relief as I expected. What I did feel was as if something dark was on the horizon, just waiting to crush my hopes. A shudder rolled through me like a spider walking down my spine. This hex wouldn't give in without a fight. The shadow of death on my soul was growing. I could sense it, whether I wanted to admit it or not. Perhaps it was aware of my plans to destroy it. Perhaps that was part of its defense. I only knew that the urge to hurry was racing through my veins.

"How are you going to ask him? Maybe we could make a sign or litter the ground with roses, make it romantic." Beck had been chattering nonstop since we got in the car. I only actually absorbed bits and pieces of what he was saying, but I got the gist of his question.

I shook my head. "I'm not asking him to the freaking prom, Beck."

His lips curved as the golden ball of sun began to dip over the horizon, streaming rays of orange onto his blue hair. "This is way more intimate."

A weird phantom of cold traveled in my chest, causing my breath to catch. And then it was gone.

"It blows my mind you think that," I managed to respond, rubbing a hand over the spot between my breasts.

He shrugged. "You'd be surprised the power blood can have on us."

I didn't want to know, and yet, I didn't have a choice in the matter. I was going to find out how important blood could be. Ironic, since it was why I was in this mess to begin with.

But seriously, how was I going to ask Torent for his blood? I don't know why I was suddenly stressing about it. He would gladly give me a gallon of his blood if it meant saving me. Why was I having such a hard time digesting the way he felt about me?

I should be rejoicing or some shit.

～

I took the weekend to marinate on the whole I-need-your-demon-blood thing and decided I would ask Torent face to face on Monday. It was the kind of request that required a personal touch, no hiding behind a text.

Odd thing was, Torent seemed to be avoiding me. I didn't want to come across as the clingy girlfriend, but it was unusual for him to flat-out ignore my texts.

My whole weekend was blah. I felt out of touch and disoriented, and I didn't know if that was because of the situation or if the hex was affecting me. But by Monday, I was going stir-crazy and dying to get out of the house.

I was eager for the week to start. Said no teenager ever. Case in point. Something was truly wrong with me.

Mine was one of the first cars to swing into the parking lot, which meant I had time to kill. Time was not my friend. My knee bounced while I let the car idle, keeping the heat on low so my bones didn't freeze.

When most of the lot was filled, I took another sweeping glance for Torent's Jeep. Had I missed him somehow? Digging out my phone, I sent him another text to join the twenty other unanswered ones I'd typed since Friday after leaving Mrs. Augustine.

My insecurities were rearing their ugly heads. *This was one of the reasons you hadn't wanted to date*, I reminded myself. *Your heart gets crushed when he inevitably disappoints you.*

But I'd thought Torent was different. He had me convinced he was not just any other guy. Then why was he giving me the cold shoulder? Why had he suddenly dropped off the face of the earth? Had he finally given up on me? Or maybe all he had ever wanted was sex. Well, he had gotten it and now was no longer interested.

The game of chase was over.

And I was the one left to pick up the pieces.

I exhaled sharply, leaning my cheek against the chilled window. *Calm down. You're jumping to conclusions. You don't know what's happening. Maybe he lost his phone.*

That was it. He must have lost his phone.

Exiting the car, I joined the masses herding into the building, all the while keeping my eyes peeled for Torent and his Jeep. The sinking feeling in my stomach was becoming heavier. Skipping my locker, I headed down the hall toward his, hoping to catch him before the bell rang. I continued to watch my peers rush down the halls and tried to muster up courage. *You can do this, Mal. There is no way Torent would refuse. No. Way.*

The problem was, he was nowhere to be found.

The bell rang, and a hole formed in my chest. It wasn't like Torent to run off to class without seeing me first. Had I become dependent on him always being there without even knowing it? I put on this I-don't-need-a-guy front, but deep down I relied on him.

My internal alarm was telling me something was wrong, but my brain was telling me not to be a clingy girlfriend, so I brushed it off, consoling myself it wasn't a big deal. I'd catch up with him in class or at lunch.

Wrong.

By the end of the day, I realized Torent hadn't shown up to school today. He was taking a mental health day. Nothing unusual about that, but I felt as if I was scrabbling at excuses for what my gut was warning me.

Two more days went by with no word from Torent. He wasn't at school. He didn't answer my calls. Or respond to my texts. All of which caused my worry to quadruple.

Something was wrong. Torent only had a week of school before finals, and then he would have the credits to graduate. He wouldn't jeopardize that unless something was seriously wrong.

Beck came up behind me and draped an arm around my shoulders. "This has gone on for long enough. You've been moping around all week. Have you forgotten about the cake?"

I cringed at our secret word for the blood hex. My feet kept slowly walking down the hall toward my locker. "How am I supposed to ask for his help if he is ignoring me?"

"It doesn't make any sense. Why would Torent be avoiding you? He loooooves you." If hearts could shine in someone's eyes, they would be glimmering in Beck's as he drew out the word love. He was such a sucker for romance.

A frown pulled at my lips. "How should I know? He won't take my calls."

Beck squeezed my shoulder. "I guess then we make him talk to you."

"Just how do you propose we do that? And before you suggest kidnapping, the answer is no. That's off the table, not even a suggestion," I said, already anticipating where his thoughts would go.

An ironic twist appeared on his lips. "God, your mind is dark."

I angled my head to the side. "Are you telling me that wasn't what you were thinking?"

Removing his arm on my shoulders, he adjusted the bag on his back, lifting the strap up higher. "I plead the fifth."

"I'm not looking to join my father in jail."

"Good point," he conceded, after rolling the idea around for a few breaths.

I grabbed Beck's hand and pulled him faster through the hallway, heading away from the lockers. Twinkles of Christmas stars glittered over our heads, the school in full holiday spirit. "Come on."

His footsteps were quick to match my strides. "I take it we're no longer going to get tacos?"

How could he think of food at a time like this?

"We're going to his house," I declared, feeling alive for the first time in days. It was time I acted. My brooding days were over. No more feeling sorry for myself. "He can't avoid me forever. If I did something to upset him, then he can be man enough to tell me to my face." We raced out of the doors and into the parking lot.

"Damn straight. Get it, girl," Beck cheered.

I rolled my eyes. "Just get in the car."

"Are we going to make it back before lunch ends?"

"Probably not."

Beck thought over what I was requesting of him, skipping classes and who knows what else. "Let's do this," he finally said with purpose. "I'm your emotional support. Detention can suck it. My friend's sanity is on the line. That trumps perfect attendance."

I don't know what I would do without a friend like Beck.

# CHAPTER 13

Skipping my afternoon classes was becoming a bad pattern I was going to need to break . . . once I rid myself of death.

"We can always grab tacos after," Beck offered, a compromise on getting food.

My appetite might be shot, but Beck was a bottomless taco pit. The shifter could eat every day, all day, and I wasn't about to stand in between him and tacos.

"Sure. We'll confront Torent and then bury my problems with Mexican food."

"Drama queen much?" Beck murmured, making himself comfortable in the passenger seat.

I shot him a glare as my car stopped at the main road. "I think I'm entitled to a moment of self-pity."

Looking left and right, I bit my lower lip. Some impatient junior with road rage honked at me.

"Why aren't we moving?" Beck asked, staring at me.

I glanced in my rearview mirror to see a line of cars starting to pile up behind me.

"I don't know where he lives," I admitted, realizing I'd never been to Torent's house before. If I was going to be his girlfriend, I needed to step up my game.

His nose wrinkled in his disbelief face. "How is that possible?" He shook his head. "Never mind. Make a left and hit the gas before the angry mob behind us decides to get hostile."

Punching the gas, I whipped the car to the left. I was a bundle of nerves when we pulled up to the Starks' house. And what a freaking house. Torent seemed to have failed to mention his family was loaded, not that it mattered to me.

A combination of burnt bricks and mahogany wood covered the exterior of the house. Bright windows lined the two stories. A three-car garage curved around the side of the house. I parked my car behind a Jeep similar to Torent's but was a cherry red with plates that read FLAMIN.

Cute.

"Do you want me to come in with you?" Beck asked, breaking the silence that had descended.

My eyes swung from the house to Beck. "I can't go into the demon's den alone."

I was pretty sure the Starks were mostly civilized, but it couldn't hurt to bring a wolf just in case.

He let out a squeal of delight. "I've been dying to get inside Torent's bedroom since the fifth grade."

Together we walked up to the front door. I wiped my sweaty palms on my jeans, telling myself I had nothing to be nervous about. There would be a reasonable explanation for Torent ghosting me. I really wanted there to be a reasonable explanation, one that wasn't him breaking up with me.

My lungs tightened. Holy crap. I was petrified he didn't care about me anymore. I had let myself fall hopelessly in love with him. If he rejected me, it would do more than sting. It would crush my heart into a million tiny pieces.

A part of me wanted to dash back to my car and run home. If I didn't confront him, I could avoid the rejection, but it wouldn't change the torment of not knowing. That would continue to plague me.

So here I was. Still in the same predicament, and I couldn't forget I needed Torent's blood.

"Have you changed your mind?"

Beck's voice jerked me out of my head. It was a dark and dangerous place to be at the moment. No more overthinking or overanalyzing. It was time for action.

Schooling my face into a neutral expression, I extended my arm and pressed the fancy iron doorbell. What would I find behind the door of a demon's house? Dungeons? Black candles? Shag carpet? Chains? To be fair, his mom was human. It had to take a brave and confident woman to marry and make a life with a demon.

I steeled my chin. It wouldn't matter what I found behind this door, only that I saw Torent.

I might be scared shitless to meet his father, but nothing about Torent frightened me, other than losing him. Still, I really, really didn't want his father to answer the door. Mr. Stark was a different level of supe.

*Relax. He's probably at work.*

Footsteps sounded from the other side, followed by a deep voice that was muffled by the thick wood between us.

What kind of job did a demon have? Lawyer? Drug lord? Executioner?

Judging by the looks of their house, papa demon made good money doing whatever unethical thing it was he did with his days . . . or nights.

I was being stereotypical, but it was because I was nervous as hell.

The door opened, and I held my breath, waiting to see whose face would appear. Torent? His father? Or . . .

My mouth went dry.

Or neither.

A young guy answered the door. He was shirtless, his jogger pants hugging low at his hips. A fine sheet of gleaming sweat glistened on his skin, as if I'd interrupted his workout. My eyes ran up the bare chest to a face that was equally as impressive as the flat abs. He leaned a lazy hand on the doorway, regarding me with a lopsided grin and a twinkle of wickedness in his violet eyes. They looked so much like Torent's that my heart cartwheeled. Those eyes collided with mine.

"Please tell me you're too old to be selling cookies," he said in a deep, hypnotic voice that made my cheeks flush.

"Hey, Zaren," Beck purred as he stepped out from behind me.

Zaren lifted a brow.

"Beck," he greeted. His eyes were quick to flicker back to me.

Zaren was one of Torent's roguish older brothers. Where Torent's hair was dark as sin, this Stark had streaks of auburn woven into his locks.

I cleared my throat. "Is Torent here?"

Zaren folded his arms like he had all the time in the world. "You must be the girl. My little bro always did have good taste."

"In girls or cookies?" I chided.

Those full lips spread into a smile that would make girls everywhere tremble. And he had the Stark dimples. Damn them.

"Both," he replied, those dimples flashing on either side of his cheeks.

Beck might swoon next to me. His hand landed on my shoulder to steady himself.

"Dear God," he whispered under his breath.

I shook off the dazzling effect from Zaren's grin and blinked. "So, is he here or not?"

"Sadly, he is not, but I am sure he is going to be disappointed he missed you."

My heart sank. If he wasn't here, then where the hell was he?

"Do you know when he'll be back?" I asked, doing my best to not sound desperate . . . and probably failing miserably.

Zaren's sparkling eyes dulled. "He's been avoiding you, hasn't he?"

I nodded.

"My brother is an idiot." Zaren opened the door wider and gestured Beck and me to come in. Together we stepped over the threshold. "I don't entirely know what my baby brother is up to, other than it was important. He left Friday in a hurry and gave us few details."

Why would he leave without saying goodbye? It didn't make sense. This sucked.

"If you talk to him, could you tell him I stopped by?"

"Sure, love."

"You have no idea where he went?" Beck inquired.

Zaren shook his head. "I wish I could help."

"He isn't in danger, is he?" The question sprang from my lips.

"With Torent, it's hard to say, but if he was in any real danger, I would know. My brother might be reckless at times, but he is smart. He would reach out to one of us for help." Zaren seemed so confident in the fact that Torent was alive and safe that he left little room for argument.

The problem was, I wanted to argue, to demand he call Torent and let me speak to him, but I refused to succumb to the title of desperate girlfriend.

"Thank you," I said to Zaren. "Will you tell him I came by?"

Zaren grinned. "Of course."

Leaving the Starks' house with virtually nothing, I felt worse. I turned in the car, angling my body inward and blurted out to Beck, "Now what? Got any brilliant ideas?"

My best friend looked at me, his brows creasing together. "Road trip?"

"We don't have the faintest idea where to begin looking."

"Shit." Beck cursed. "We could ask Zaren for his blood. He's not his brother, but he's mostly a decent guy and half demon. Ticks off all the qualifications."

Very true. And I should have probably marched back up to the house and asked him to come into the woods with me so I could use his blood to break a hex. I wouldn't sound crazy at all. At the moment, I didn't care about my mental state. But asking Zaren would mean explaining why I needed his blood, and I didn't want to have to go into the long-winded story of my family's history.

So that left me at a crossroads.

My foot tapped on the floor of my car. Without demon blood, I was screwed. If word got out about my hex to the Court of the Sun and the Moon, the rulers over the supernaturals . . . I shuddered to think what would happen.

# CHAPTER 14

*J* stayed in bed through dinner that night, unable to muster an appetite. Mom and Gigi didn't pester me about my sullen mood, and I was relieved. I wouldn't be able to get the words out without losing my shit.

With Torent gone, I had to devise a backup plan. Soon. A shadow of darkness swirling inside me was growing stronger, digging its phantom claws into my soul. I was spiraling down a dark hole.

Near bedtime, a soft knock sounded on my door.

"Mal? Honey? Are you okay?" It was Mom.

I rolled over in my bed and closed my eyes, evening out my breathing. The door creaked open, and I continued to pretend I was asleep, saying nothing. After a few moments, she shut the door and padded quietly down the hall to her own room.

I lay awake until past midnight, contemplating my options and trying not to let my emotions get the best of me. Round and round I went—an endless circle. I had to undo the hex. To do that, I needed demon blood. The only viable option was to ask a complete stranger. Zaren was my best shot.

*Shit. Shit. Shit.*

Frustration stung at my eyes, a film of tears blocking my vision as my fist hit the pillow, taking out all my aggression and misery.

When I'd exerted myself and felt no better, I pressed my face into the pillow, a bone-deep sadness coming over me.

The dried tears were replaced by a dull ache behind my eyes. Then came the anger. It was so intense my body was vibrating. This was my father's fault. If I hadn't hated him before, I did so now with a fervent loathing.

Morning stirred before I got the chance to sleep, and getting out of bed was a chore—one I didn't want to do. To rise would mean I had to deal with the fact it was time I told Mom what was wrong. She and Gigi were already suspicious and knew something was bothering me. They were watching me.

Mom came into the room, and I was still in bed with the covers pulled over my head, shutting out the sunshine. Who needed light when I was filled with nothing but darkness?

She sat on the edge of the bed, and the mattress dipped under her weight. With gentle hands, she peeled back a corner of the blanket.

I squinted and groaned. My body sunk into the bed like it was a tanker truck loaded with iron. Everything hurt. My head. My bones. My muscles. My heart. I had no energy to move and barely enough to open my eyes, but I forced them to part.

Concern flickered in her thickly lashed eyes. "Rough couple of days, huh?"

My gaze took her in. She looked good, the best I'd ever seen her. Her skin was creamy, soft, and flawless. The dark circles and light wrinkles were missing from around her eyes, and there was even a rosy flush to her cheeks. I nodded, my throat closing up. She was happy, and I wasn't ready to be the one who put the shadow of gloom into her eyes. She had enough of it in her life.

"You want to talk about it yet?"

*Yes. Yes. Yes.*

My emotions screamed.

I shook my head. "It's just cramps and a headache."

We both knew it was bullshit. She kissed my forehead, tucking my hair behind my ear as she studied my face. "Take a mental health day. Work through what is bothering you, and if you want to talk tonight, I'll listen. You never know, I might even have some solid advice for the first time ever in your life."

I forced what could pass for a smile. "Thanks, Mom."

Giving my hand a squeeze, she eased to her feet, but paused in the archway leading into the hall and glanced over her shoulder. "Things are turning around for us. I never thought that Havenwood Falls would be home again, but it always was."

Mom needed me to be happy, so I gave her the best encouraging smile I could, not wanting her to spend her day worrying about me when she needed to be concentrating on her job. She was content. For the first time in her life, it wasn't because of a guy. How could I burst her bubble?

I made the decision to keep my secret a little bit longer. I'd take the day to nurse my broken heart, then the time to feel sorry for myself came to end.

~

Curled up on the couch with one of Gigi's knitted blankets in the colors of the sea, I sat in front of the TV, watching reality trash. It made me feel slightly better about my own life . . . just a smidge.

Gigi was out doing volunteer work at the local animal shelter. Once a month she dedicated her day to helping Isa Hilton, the local vet and owner of the shelter, with the stray and abandoned animals of Havenwood Falls. I was grateful to have the house to myself.

An hour went by, and I hadn't budged from my spot on the couch, not even an inch, and I was satisfied to stay here for the rest of the day, doing nothing but watching mindless entertainment. I must have dozed off for a little bit, the lack of sleep finally catching up to me.

I dreamed.

I dreamed I was walking through my house, down the carpeted hallway into the kitchen. Something was off about the way I moved. It was me but it wasn't me. I didn't know how else to explain the feeling of knowing your body moved but you weren't controlling its movements.

Stopping in the middle of the kitchen, I twisted my wrist in the air, and a knife from the butcher block wiggled before unsheathing itself completely. The blade hung in the air level with my nose.

So simple. It had been like snapping my fingers, summoning the knife to do as I bid. The power I wielded often frightened me. In my dreams, none of that fear lived, only a desire for more. My power filled me with the strength and roaring of the sea.

I smiled, twirling the blade in circles.

*Knock. Knock.*

My eyes glanced at the hallway that led to the front door. Someone was there. Who could it be? This was a dream, after all. The grin on my lips widened.

*Knock. Knock. Knock.*

Knuckles rapped against the front door in a more persistent rhythm.

I glided down the hallway with the floating blade in tow. This version of me had a thing for knives. I didn't like how I was feeling inside, the strange elation swimming in my veins. Something wasn't right about it. Something foul was at play. Something dark loomed inside of me.

I closed my fingers over the doorknob without looking outside, but when my hand touched the metal, a surge of heat pulsed from the other side of the door. I hesitated, my hand paused on the knob. The glint of the silver blade at the corner of my eyes reminded me I had nothing to fear. I wasn't powerless or defenseless.

I brought the hovering knife forward, so it would stand between whoever was behind the door and me. One hell of a warm greeting.

My fingers fumbled with the locks, and I whipped open the door, expecting to see the face of my father or someone equally menacing. Instead, a white light burned around the figure, making it impossible for me to see their face.

What the hell? What was this?

Rotating my fingers in the air, I commanded the knife to move forward, closer to the flickering form radiating heat in waves.

"Show yourself," I demanded.

"Mallory," the light spoke my name.

I cocked my head to the side, regarding the figure. Was it dangerous?

*Yes,* a dark voice in my head replied. *Eliminate.*

The blade was still in the air, just waiting for me to give the order. One quick twitch and it would be over. Blood would spill.

"Mallory," the voice behind the blinding light shouted.

It was so familiar . . . yet, I couldn't recall the face the voice belonged to, or a name.

My shoulders shook. I looked away as the light grew brighter, blinking. Color swirled behind my eyelids. Then it burst, leaving me shrouded in darkness. My breath came out in short pants, the sound echoing in my ears.

"Mallory?" a gentle voice whispered.

I blinked, realizing my eyes had been shut, hence the darkness. My hand gripped onto the doorframe as I steadied myself, trying to make sense of what was happening. The sun warmed my face from the open door, and a cool breeze blew over my cheeks.

I went rigid when I noticed the blade hovering a few feet in front of me, and I paled seeing who it was pointed at. Torent. He glowered, staring at me with an odd expression. My mind blanked, then I was assaulted with an onslaught of emotions.

"Torent," I sighed, staring at the half demon.

The blade clattered to the floor as my power whooshed out of me. What had I done? What happened to me? I hadn't been dreaming, I'd been sleepwalking, and what I could have done . . . It scared the crap out of me.

"Hey, it's okay. You're safe." His hands framed my face. I hadn't noticed until then that I was trembling.

I cast my eyes downward to where the knife lay on the ground. "I could have killed you. Oh, my God. I almost killed you."

The voice. It had coaxed me, wanted me to hurt him.

His thumb brushed over my cheek. "But you didn't."

My gaze lifted, colliding with his. He was here. I launched myself into his arms.

His arms swooped around me, and the tension in his muscles relaxed against my body. A long whoosh of breath left his chest, and he clung to me for minutes, as if he was never going to let me go.

I had so much to say to him, but I held Torent, allowing myself the immense pleasure of being in his arms. He smelled as I remembered, woodsy with a hint of mint.

After some time, he pulled back to look down at my face, and the first thing I noticed was his eyes. They were more violet than gold, but the flecks of his powers lingered.

"Where the hell have you been?" The high of seeing him alive and in the flesh faded, leaving me with a million questions. "Do you have any idea what you put me through this week?"

His face nuzzled the side of my cheek. "I'm sorry," he murmured.

Lacing our fingers together, I tugged him inside. "Why didn't you call me?"

His eyes shifted to our joined hands before looking back up. "Where I went, cell phones don't exist. I never would have gotten a signal. It wasn't until I returned to Havenwood Falls that my phone sent through all the messages."

"You left Havenwood Falls? Why?"

"For you. I had to do something to help."

My lips pressed into a thin line. "And you didn't think you should have told me before you left?"

"But then you would have talked me out of it," he explained casually. "I would have stayed if you asked, and I needed to at least try to find a way to break the hex."

I crossed my arms, about to tell him I'd already figured out a way to break the curse, but I angled my head to the side. "Where did you go?"

"It isn't important. I got nothing useful, just the ramblings of a trapped man."

"You went to see my father?" I guessed, knowing it was like Torent to go directly to the source, screw all the red tape.

He didn't deny or confirm, but said, "I'd do anything for you . . . even risk death itself."

Dammit. Why did he have to go and do that, get all mushy on me? I wanted to stay annoyed at him, but how could I?

"What did he say?" I hated myself for even asking. Did I really care what my father had said?

"Most of it didn't make sense, but he did say something about a mark of death. How your mother wanted to take you from him, and he found a way to ensure that never happened. With this mark, he'd always have a connection to you."

I gulped. My father had done this to me—he had cursed me. I'd had my suspicions, but to hear it confirmed . . . It made me sick to my stomach. Sympathy shone in his eyes as I met his gaze. He hated being the bearer of such devastating news, but sometimes the truth hurt, and to be honest, my father had been dead to me most of my life. I wasn't going to let him win.

"I appreciate you wanting to help me, but Beck and I found a spell that might break the hex. At least, Mrs. Augustine thinks so."

His brows arched. "Mrs. Augustine, the teacher?"

I nodded. "She's a witch."

Leaning a shoulder against the wall, the corner of his lip tipped up. "I know. I'm just surprised you sought her help. Smart."

"It was Beck's idea," I supplied, giving credit where credit was due.

Torent shoved his hands into his front pockets. "I have to give it to the shifter. He's handy to have around."

"There's just one thing," I added, biting my lip. "I need your blood."

"My blood?" he echoed, a hint of incredulity glinting in his violet eyes.

I gave him the rundown of the spell Mrs. Augustine believed would free me of the darkness, of what I needed to do and where.

The light shifted in his eyes. "Magic always finds a way to

balance the light with the dark. If it is my blood you need, I will gladly give you a pint, but . . . I want something in return."

I was taken a little aback by his request for something in return, and my expression slackened. "What did you have in mind?"

He twirled a strand of my hair around his finger. "Go with me to the winter dance."

A dance? Why was he talking about a dance? It took me a few breaths to catch up. "The Cold Moon Ball? Do you really think that is a good idea right now? My life is complicated. I don't see how going to a dance is going to fix what is happening to me. The hex won't give me a night off. In fact, it's probably a bad idea. What if something happens?"

"It's my last one before I graduate, and I want to spend it with you, if only for a few hours. You deserve to have fun, Mal." He put his finger to my lips before I could protest again. "And it falls on the full moon."

That got my attention. The full moon was when Mrs. Augustine would perform the spell, the lunar phase of the moon being at its height of energy.

"I'll go with you, but I'm warning you. You might not leave with all your toes." I was a swimmer, not a dancer.

His response was a dimpled grin, full of wickedness.

# CHAPTER 15

$\mathcal{T}$he night of the Cold Moon Ball also happened to be the winter solstice. It was convenient—the perfect cover. While the town celebrated the winter solstice, Beck, Torent, and I would be sneaking off to meet Mrs. Augustine in the woods near Peacock Lake. I promised Torent a dance, but then the *fun* really began.

The day. The time. The place. It was all set into motion. We were to meet Mrs. Augustine around eight o'clock to get everything we needed in order. When the moon was at its highest point, she would cast her spell, and I'd drink the magical concoction.

And it wasn't a moment too soon.

From the time I'd woken up this morning, my world felt off-kilter. Although I couldn't pinpoint what was making me feel so foreign in my own body, I told myself to get through the night. As long as I didn't have another sleepwalking episode, it would be all over by tomorrow, and I could go back to living my life, concentrating on things like graduating, swimming, and Torent.

To have a normal life with a hot guy—such an alien concept, especially since he was anything but average.

Beck had dragged me to every shop in Havenwood Falls the weekend before the big town celebration, something I dreaded as much as what would happen during the dance. Some girls loved makeup, hair, and frilly dresses. Then there were girls like me.

"Why did I let him talk me into this?" I mumbled to myself. I was alone in my room, trying to wiggle into an organza gown of baby blue and white. "What was wrong with yoga pants and a sports bra?" Talking to myself was my way of dealing with crap I didn't want to face. And tonight was a double whammy.

Dancing and a hex.

Go me.

The last thing I wanted to do was get ready for a party. My palms were sweaty. My stomach was close to heaving with nerves. And my hair wouldn't cooperate to save my life.

The silver-blue sparkly and sheer material looked itchy, but I was surprised to find it didn't irritate my skin. Slipping my arms into the straps, I found the bodice was slimming and silky with teal jewels that resembled flurries of snowflakes. Mom had managed to salvage my hair, sweeping it up onto the crown of my head, a tiny braid curving around the base of the hair tie. Blond curls cascaded over my shoulders. When she brought out the sparkle hairspray, I nearly chucked it into the garbage, but Mom was in her element, having the time of her life dolling me up. Since we were both feeling emotional and sentimental for two entirely different reasons, I only sighed, crossed my arms, and let her work her magic.

"There, all done," she said, smiling pleasantly at me in the vanity mirror. Putting the cap back onto the soft pink lipstick she had applied to my lips, Mom stood up. "Go have a look," she encouraged, gesturing to the full-length mirror in the corner of my room.

I stepped in front of my reflection, taking in the glittering material like woven snowy stars as it draped to the floor. My gaze connected to the aqua eyes in the mirror, framed with thick black lashes and shimmering eye shadow of smoke with hints of teal. A silver snowflake charm hung from a ribbon choker around my slender neck. I didn't have words for the woman who stared back at me. She was a dream. I was afraid to look too deeply, for, behind the awe, darkness ascended.

"You've never looked more beautiful, Mallory." Mom swept a curl off my shoulder, a mist of tears in her eyes.

Something was in the air, other than perfume, hairspray, and glitter. Perhaps it was the reenactment I had looming in front of me, the worst night in Mom's life and the moment that shaped mine. We were both sappy. I hugged her.

"I don't know what I would do without you," I admitted.

She flicked the end of my nose. "Right back at you, kid."

Growing up, I never felt like I was Mom's top priority. It always seemed as if she was chasing some kind of happiness that didn't really involve me, but I understood now. She had been trying to forget the past, not forget me. I knew she loved me, but now I felt loved.

The ball was a blur of people in fancy attire, twinkling lights, strumming music, and delicate cuisine. Not even the numerous weddings I'd attended, mostly Mom's, held a candle to the Cold Moon Ball. I lingered at Torent's side, my hand looped through his arm. I tried to smile, to have a good time for Torent's sake, but what we were going to do later in the night plagued my thoughts.

I only had to survive another hour. In my current state of mind, it felt like a lifetime.

"Relax," Torent whispered in my ear.

The skirt of my dress floated lightly around me as Torent and I strolled through the grounds.

"This is me relaxed," I said through my teeth.

His soft chuckle warmed against my neck. "Have I told you how breathtaking you look?"

Only a dozen times, but I didn't mind. Torent looked equally impressive in all black. He forwent the traditional tux for jeans, a button-down shirt, and a vest. I still had a hard time comprehending that this dashing male was my boyfriend.

"How about we skip the dance and go straight to making out in your car?" I proposed.

"Don't tempt me." The huskiness of his voice curled around me like a magnetic hug, pulling me closer to him.

That was the thing. I wanted to tempt him. And I wanted to stop my brain from hashing over what was still to come. My eyes connected with his, and a craving unfurled inside me. It was moments like this when it became so clear that we belonged together. My soul knew it.

"What can I do to change your mind?"

His hands slipped to my waist, and he leaned toward me, his jaw grazing my cheek. Tingles radiated from my heart, and my pulse quickened. His breath was warm and intoxicating. I arched up on my toes to press—

"What up, lovebirds?" Beck sauntered up to us with a stupid grin on his face. His wolfish silver eyes were beaming under the moonlight—the cold moon. It was fitting for my best friend. He never looked more alive, more in his element. The lapels of his navy velvet blazer were accentuated by the hues of his hair.

I found it difficult to be miffed at him for interrupting what could have been a blissful moment of peace only found in Torent's arms.

"Look at you," I said, my eyes taking him in fully from head to toe. Unraveling myself from Torent's hold, I went and gave Beck a hug. "You look amazing."

"Likewise, chica. We're all set for tonight," he murmured near my ear before pulling away.

I nodded, feeling that pesky lump return in my chest. It would follow me until this night was over and the hex banished.

Beck's eyes scanned the bash. "Have you eaten?" he asked.

I shook my head. "I don't think I can."

Beck clucked his tongue, his eyes sharpening. "Mal, you need your strength."

"He's right," Torent added, the two of them ganging up on me. "Come on, let's get some food."

Torent met Beck's gaze, and a silent exchange passed between them. My guess was they had made a pact to look out for me or some other macho promise.

How could I be annoyed? They cared about me, and I would have done the same for both of them.

I let them lead me to a table for four, where we were served an elaborate feast of turkey, potatoes, salad, and more food than I could possibly eat. For their sake, I made myself pick at my plate, forcing down the tasteless food. It wasn't that the appetizers, salads, and meats weren't delicious. They were probably some of the best food I'd ever had, but I couldn't enjoy the flavors.

As the ball shifted to the Mills Mansion and the crowds began to move out, Torent, Beck, and I took off in his Jeep, going the opposite direction. I glanced over my shoulder out the back window, watching the horse-drawn carriages fade in the distance.

My hands were shaking as I changed out of my fancy dress and traded my heels for boots. My attire was not fit for traipsing around the woods. Beck may have killed me if I'd gotten blood on the dress he claimed brought joy to his life.

He was such a weirdo sometimes. I couldn't help but love him.

"You ready to make magic, crash car?" Torent stated in an attempt to quiet my nerves.

Lifting my boot up on the seat, I tied the laces. "After tonight, I'm taking a break from this supernatural stuff."

"I'd say you earned it."

Our drive toward Peacock Lake was short from the center of town. Torent got as close as we could get by car; the rest of the way we would be trekking through the woods.

The three of us slunk off into the snow-dusted trees. The land itself seemed empty, as if the plants and animals sensed what was about to transpire and bowed to the laws of magic. Peeking through the dense branches, moonlight danced over the shadows. As we passed a small frozen stream made by the occasional melting snow during the day, Torent came to an abrupt halt. His head swung over his shoulder, and those violet eyes were tinged with glowing gold flecks.

"What is it?" I asked when he didn't say anything but continued to stare into the dark trees behind us, searching for something.

"I'm not sure. I can't shake the feeling we're being followed." His body was tight.

"Who would be that dumb?" Beck pointed out, but he turned in the same direction and let his inner wolf peek out, eyes glowing silver. "The wind would be stagnant tonight of all nights," he grumbled. "I can't pick up a scent."

"It could be nothing. Let's keep moving. We're not far."

My boots snapped and crunched twigs and frosty blades of grass. As we drew closer to Peacock Lake, I became alive. I had no other way to describe the sudden tingles in my blood, the splash of waves in my ears, or the pull deep in the marrow of my bones. I inhaled, letting the crisp air burn my lungs. Being here, close to the lake, had somehow eased the dread that pitted in my gut.

We came to a fork in the path. One led to Peacock Lake, the other toward the greater falls. The vision Styx had given me was of a clearing hedged with various conifers and wild shrubs.

"Which way?" Beck asked as our eyes bounced between the two paths.

The trees to my right seemed to bend outward, forming an arch into an invisible path I couldn't see. I blinked, and it was gone.

"This way," I said, not waiting for either of them to object, and I took neither path, but veered into a section of the woods intertwined in a thick weave of untamed pines and snow-covered oaks and elm trees. Snow crunched under my feet as I pushed forward until the thicket gave way to the cultivated glade.

A flock of black birds soared out of the tree canopy.

"That wasn't ominous in the slightest," Beck said dryly, breaking the silence.

Magic seemed to tremble in the air, and the clearing felt ancient, a place of great natural power that existed long before humans walked the earth. Moonlight shone over the ice-tipped grass, making the glade appear like glass, enchanting and fragile. The three of us stood on the edge, taking in the wonder of this place. It was impossible not to feel it, human or supe.

Beck checked the time and his phone, after scanning the towering and thick trees for Mrs. Augustine. "She should be here already," he muttered.

Puffs of cold air exhaled from my lungs, and I wrapped my arms around myself. *Please don't let anything go wrong.*

"You're cold," Torent stated. "Beck, be a gentleman and give her your jacket.

"I'm fine," I chattered, convincing no one.

Beck came up beside me and draped the warm, velvety coat over my shoulders. "That's better," he said, rubbing his hands over my arms to encourage blood flow.

"You're late," a woman's voice sounded from the shadows. Mrs. Augustine emerged, the frost-tipped grass crunching under her feet. She too had been at the Cold Moon Ball but had slipped away a half hour before us. Her dress was a deep red, popping against the white-dusted trees and ground.

"Is everything in place?" Torent asked, forgoing pleasantries and taking charge. Crispness had entered his tone, making his words sound clipped. He wanted to get this over with. We had that in common.

"I just need the blood." Her voice was different from what she used in the classroom. Gone was the teacher. The woman who stood in front of us was every inch the witch. Energy tingled in the air around her.

At the sudden reminder of what was going to transpire here, I felt the blood drain from my face, and my stomach twisted.

Torent joined our hands. "Let's get the show on the road."

# CHAPTER 16

*M*rs. Augustine stood inside a charred circle as if she had burned it into the ground. Since she made no move to leave the ring, the three of us joined her in the middle. My eyes immediately went to the sacred blade in her hand.

*Son of a bitch.*

I gulped, and Torent's hand tightened in mine.

"It's going to be okay," he murmured.

Mrs. Augustine handed the blade to Torent first. "Remember, I must do the spell when the moon is at its highest, giving us just under an hour. We don't have time to waste."

Torent released my hand and took the offered dagger without blinking. He flipped it over his hand, making a smooth slit across his palm as if he'd done it a million times before. Not even a flicker of pain shone in his expression. As he clenched his fist, the blood flowed, dripping into an iron goblet Mrs. Augustine had brought with her. The drip, drip, drip of Torent's blood hitting metal had my stomach pitching.

I closed my eyes and took a deep breath.

"You'd make the worst vamp," Beck joked. He was standing on the other side of me, assuming a supportive stance identical to Torent's.

"I'm still not convinced you're an actual wolf," Torent said, before turning to me. "Your turn, love." The encouraging smile on his lips warmed my cold blood slightly, and the endearment helped.

I nodded, my eyes shifting to the knife he held out. My fingers trembled as I wrapped them around the cool and smooth hilt. The wood was heavier than I'd expected. The dagger shook as I clenched it tighter, bringing it to lie over the inside of my palm. My fingers curled over the blade, and all I had to do was pull it out. I inhaled, my lips trembling, and the world seemed to hold its breath with me, going still.

"I-I can't do it. Here," I quailed, unfurling my hand and outstretching the dagger to Torent. "You do it."

"Are you sure?"

I shoved out my hand. "Yes," I whispered, squeezing my eyes shut while I waited for the pain.

It was quick, a surprise sting that startled me more than hurt, and was followed by a gentle squeezing of my hand. I didn't open my eyes until Torent pressed a kiss to the center of my palm.

"All done," he murmured.

My lashes fluttered, and I found myself captured in a sea of violet starlight. His eyes held mine and steadied my pulse.

"Thank you," I mouthed.

He only gave a slight incline of his head before turning toward Mrs. Augustine, who was waiting at the heart of her spellbound circle. Taking the goblet with both hands, she tilted her head to the moon and the stars.

*"To the winds of change, I call thee tonight.*
*To the spirits from the other side, I summon thee to me.*
*Shift the source of illness borne.*
*Unleash the power hidden from day, in the night so deep.*
*Blood to blood, as I will so mote it be."*

Her words were harmonious, ringing over the glade with conviction, and the wind picked up, howling like a banshee as it blew at my back, sending my hair flying in a cluster of chaos.

Torent's hand was my anchor. I held onto him tight, praying.

And then silence descended. Nothing moved or stirred, as if the elements surrounding us respected what had been summoned.

"It's done," she said, offering me the cup.

I dared to look inside, unsure what I would find. The dark liquid swirled like sparkling cranberry juice. *Not so bad*, I told myself, lifting the glass.

"Bottoms up," I mumbled. The cool metal of the rim pressed to my lips, and I tipped my head back, ready to—

A rustling of leaves and branches sounded from the edge of the tree line, and both Beck and Torent went on alert, their bodies hardening. I licked my lips, lowering the goblet.

"Did you come alone?" Mrs. Augustine demanded, her eyes narrowing.

Torent's body had gone tight beside me, and a low snarl erupted from Beck's throat like an animal.

"Yes. We told no one," Beck assured, but Torent and him sharing a look, and I wondered if they too were remembering that feeling of being watched in the woods.

"And you weren't followed?" our teacher reiterated.

Torent's eyes were glowing as he scanned through the shadows and thicket. "Not that we know of."

"I wouldn't be so sure about that," Mrs. Augustine warned, a hawk-like expression hardening her face.

"Beck." Torent gave a slight tilt of his head, giving a command.

A complete shocker to me, my best friend obeyed, and before I comprehended what was happening, Beck had undressed and shifted into a beast. Gray fur replaced his creamy skin. Silver eyes sparkled under moonlight. I'd never seen Beck in his other form. He was majestic, his lean body stronger as a wolf.

Keeping low to the ground, Beck padded over to the trees where we had emerged not long ago, using his keen senses to sniff out any unwelcome visitors. Paw prints stamped the frosty ground. His ears went back, a low growl rumbling deep in his throat.

Then he lunged, disappearing into the darkness of the woods.

Twigs snapped and crispy leaves crunched, but I could see nothing. The wrestling was shortly followed by a female squeal.

I knew that voice.

Beck was dragging out the intruder by the hem of a beautiful red satin dress, snarling through his clenched jaws.

Oh, for the love of everything holy!

"Brooklyn?" Torent's voice echoed over the clearing.

My fellow nymph was playing tug-of-war with Beck, fighting to get the wolf to release her dress. "Bite me, mongrel, and I'll make a fur coat out of you," Brooklyn threatened, glaring at Beck.

"What the hell are you doing here?" Torent demanded, shoving a hand into his hair.

She gave one hard yank, and Beck chose that moment to release his locked grip, letting gravity take over. Brooklyn's arms went flailing in the air as she fell backward on her ass with an audible oomph. Red-faced with rage, Brooklyn clenched her fists in the ground. If it was possible, steam would have expelled from her ears, she was that spitting mad.

*Shit.*

Before Beck had the chance to put some distance between Brooklyn and himself, she shot out her hand, zapping him with a bolt of electricity.

Beck yelped, scampering backward as fast as his four legs would allow, and followed up with a growl of warning.

It was my turn to get pissed. I stepped forward in between them, forcing Brooklyn to look at me. "Try that shit again, Brooklyn, and I'll chain you to a tree."

Torent was instantly at my side. "What are you doing here?" he asked again with no less patience than the first time.

Shoving to her feet with her chin jerked upward, she brushed off the dusting of snow and dirt from her soiled dress.

"I saw the three of you leave." Her words were short and clipped.

"And you took it upon yourself to follow us. Why?" He was relentless in his tone.

Her dark blue eyes pinned me, pretty lips curling in disgust. "She's up to something, and I want to know what."

"It's none of your business. Now go, Brooklyn, before someone notices you're not at the ball," I spat.

"If it's all the same, I'd rather stay and watch the show." She threw Beck's words back at us, the little schemer.

"We don't have time to argue." Mrs. Augustine stepped forward, her voice carrying over the clearing. "Mallory, you must drink before it's too late."

I'd forgotten about the goblet clutched in my hands. Brooklyn sneered, but I ignored her. I had far more important things to deal with than her meddling in my life. In one quick motion, I threw back the contents of the cup, not allowing myself to think about the cocktail of blood and magic I was putting into my body.

"Why are you drinking spelled blood?" Brooklyn interrupted, watching me with scrutiny.

I turned to Mrs. Augustine. "How long before we know if it works?"

"The spell should banish the hex immediately."

I probably should have asked if this was going to hurt. So I waited. And waited. Four sets of eyes stared at me expectantly.

"Nothing's happening."

Beck had shifted back into his human self and was buttoning up his shirt when he asked, "Did we do something wrong?"

"There's no reason it shouldn't have worked. Mixing your blood with a demon's should have been enough to counteract the hex," Mrs. Augustine confirmed.

My chest hollowed out. "So why didn't it work?"

"You're too corrupt," Brooklyn snarled in an almost laugh.

"Why are you still here?" I snapped back, ready to slam her head into the frozen ground.

"To watch you fall on your face." Her lips grew into a pleased grin. "So you're hexed? I'd love to kiss the witch who spelled you."

The urge to cause Brooklyn bodily harm tripled, but what she had said sparked an idea. "Wait. Maybe she's onto something. Give me your blood," I ordered.

"As if I would ever stoop so low," Brooklyn squeaked. "Absolutely not. I wouldn't give you my blood even if the world depended—"

Beck tackled her to the ground. "Quick, cut the bitch."

Oh. My. God. What was even happening? This couldn't be my life.

And yet, it was.

Unlike me, Torent didn't hesitate. He snatched the dagger and pricked the tip of Brooklyn's finger.

"Ouch!" Something violent and predatory crept into her dark blue eyes. "Release me, mutt," she barked at Beck. A second later his hands jerked back in swift movements. "I'm going to dismantle you, Torent Stark!"

"She shocked me. Again," Beck proclaimed, staring at his now hairless arms. She had singed them clean off.

"You'll pay for this," Brooklyn hissed at me with hate as I crouched down to catch the blood now dripping into the goblet.

"I'm sure I will," I replied. "But if this works, I'll be in your debt."

Beck helped Brooklyn to her feet as Torent sliced his other hand, adding his blood to Brooklyn's. My fellow nymph might not be a saint, but her bloodline was as pure and good as they came. I don't know how the hell the goddess Aphrodite ever blessed someone like Brooklyn.

She fought against Beck's grip, jerking her arms with revulsion. "Let me go," she seethed.

He waited until Torent had handed the goblet over to Mrs. Augustine before releasing her.

"Behave," Beck warned.

Brooklyn's chin jutted out, her eyes blazing in the night.

Mrs. Augustine's lips formed a thin line, watching us with disapproval. "I might not agree with your methods, but you better hope this works. The spell might not be as strong as the first. All we can do is pray it's enough."

Making haste with her magic, she spoke the words, and once again I drank from the goblet, downing every last drop of the enchanted mixture.

It was warm and thicker than I remembered as I forced the blood down my throat, my nose wrinkling. I shuddered at the bitter taste. A minute went by. Then another.

Mrs. Augustine let loose a disheartened sigh.

Brooklyn laughed haughtily.

Beck swore under his breath.

And Torent and I just stared at each other.

I was about to say screw it when my breath began to come fast and hard. I panted through my teeth in what I was sure was a panic attack.

A small noise came out of Brooklyn's mouth.

"Quiet," snapped Mrs. Augustine. "Open yourself up, Mallory. Don't fight it."

Something thrummed and pulsed, rising and lashing through my blood. Something not of this world. Something old and very, very dark. The thing inside me was roiling, desperate to keep its claws gripped to my soul. It shook my body with a building force as the magic, combined with Torent and Brooklyn's blood, hunted for a way to rip off the very essence of who I was.

A rumble thundered under my feet, followed by a whoosh and a bloodcurdling scream that resonated to the stars.

My scream.

"Mallory!" My name bellowed from Torent's lips, but it was too late.

Images slammed into me, breaking the void of blackness, but as I saw them, I wished for the darkness. One after one, they rolled through my mind.

My father looming over Ryle's dead body, grinning. The pleasure killing gave him, the power he desired, expelled in the air like a toxic poison.

I saw my mother sprawled out on the forest floor, blood pooling around her, eyes vacant and gone. Gigi was beside her in a similar fashion, her long silver hair glowing under the moonlight, streaked with red.

And then there was me, standing proudly beside my father, thriving on the power he had bestowed upon me. In my right hand was the ceremonial knife, dripping with blood—my family's blood.

I shook my head.

*No. I don't want it. I don't want to be like you.*

He didn't seem to hear me, didn't so much as flinch.

*Help me! Help me, help me,* I silently begged. *Torent. Beck. Anyone.* I pounded against the darkness, tears streaming down my face. *Get me out. Please,* I pleaded.

But no one heard. No one saw the fear, the panic, the desperation swallowing me, and it became clear. I was going to have to claw my way out of the darkness, but I was frozen in place, undiluted terror keeping me prisoner.

*"Mallory,"* a voice of silk and shadows crooned.

"What do you want from me?" I screamed.

*"Accept who you are,"* it seemed to coo without actually speaking. *"My daughter."*

Rippling terror buried deep inside me, rooted my feet in place, but I refused to give in. *No,* my mind softly rejected the temptation. *I'm not just your daughter. I'm also the daughter of a goddess.*

I held on to that thought as if my life depended on it, and it a way, it did. I had no idea how long it had been since I'd drunk the potion, but for me, time seemed to have dragged, ensnaring me in my own personal hell with darkness. Each passing heartbeat, my resolve weakened, until something brushed against my hand, a touch.

I recognized that light caress.

Torent's fingers closed around my mine, joining our hands and with it, our powers. The pad of his thumb stroked over the back of my hand. It was the encouragement I needed, grounding me. I unleashed my power—the power I'd almost forgotten I possessed.

Torent and the feelings he elicited reminded me what I was capable of.

A flash of pure white light exploded behind my eyes, banishing the darkness that held me.

The light faded and I blinked, surprised to find myself on the ground, curled into Torent's arms.

He glanced down into my face, relief in his violet eyes. "Hey," he said.

"I'm going to be sick." Turning my head to the side, I vomited, but not my dinner.

A smog of black expelled out of my mouth. Blackness swirled from the night, curling around me like a mist of death, cold and evil. It poked at every inch of me with little phantom talons of smoke, looking for—no, demanding—a way back in.

"What the hell is that?" Brooklyn shrieked.

"We need to trap it before it can find another host," Mrs. Augustine informed.

Torent scooped his hands under my elbows, lifting me to my feet. He shoved me behind him, trying to stay between the shadow mist and me. "And just how do we do that?" he hissed.

"With this," Mrs. Augustine said. I took my eyes off the cloud of blackness just long enough to see her holding up an elongated glass bottle tinged in seafoam green.

"A bottle?" Torent said with incredulity. He took the bottle from Mrs. Augustine and cracked his neck. "This should be fun."

The shadow sprang from nightmares. It crawled and slunk over the ground, with no real shape or form, searching for its next victim or for me. The five of us backed away, each contemplating how the hell we were going to coax it inside the bottle in Torent's hands.

Why did it have to be him?

I should have been the one trying to capture the darkness. This was my fault, my problem.

"Anyone have a plan?" Beck mumbled. He and I were shoulder to shoulder with Torent on the other side of me.

"If I die, I swear I will haunt you," Brooklyn said to me, not taking her gaze off the shadow.

"Zap it or something," Beck snarled at Brooklyn.

"Me?" she squealed. "This is not my problem."

I refrained from rolling my eyes, afraid to take my attention off the shadow stalking us.

Torent stepped forward, putting himself in harm's way.

"What are you doing?" I pleaded.

"Taking this thing down." His voice was low and gritty. He didn't give me the chance to argue, throwing out his arms. Hellfire erupted over his body, casting an aura of amber around him. The fire crackled and popped along his skin.

Anticipating the threat, the shadow hissed right before it morphed a small section of its form into a black, gleaming talon. Torent stepped closer, and it hissed in a noise that sounded like a thousand children screaming.

It slashed out with its talon, striking Torent in the face. His head whipped to the side, the fire along his fingers and arms sputtering.

"Torent!" I cried out, my heart knocking in my chest.

He raised his head, irises glowing nearly gold. Blood oozed from under his right eye. "That wasn't very nice."

I reacted without thinking, unaware of what I was doing until a surge of power trembled out of me. No one was more surprised than me when the shadow froze under my command.

Someone gasped.

*Holy crap. It had magnetic properties.*

"Gotcha," I muttered.

Beck, Torent, and Brooklyn all pinned me with equal gazes of shock. "Are you doing this?" Torent asked, the flames of hellfire extinguished.

I nodded. "It must have particles of metal inside the shadows."

The mist shrieked, bucking against my restraint, but I held on.

"Think you can get it inside this?" Torent held up the bottle.

"Only one way to find out," I ground out, keeping my concentration wholly on the shadow.

Using my power for something good, I steered the perilous smoke straight for the bottle outstretched in Torent's hand. If I slipped up . . . If it broke free . . . I refused to think like that.

The smoke of shadows thrashed and struggled against me as I slowly began to force it to move toward us. I reinforced the power flowing through me, putting all the energy I had left in my body into trapping the curse.

"This is not how I thought my night was going to go," Brooklyn grumbled, but even when complaining, her voice had a silky threat to it.

Beads of sweat gathered at my brow, but I almost had it to the opening of the bottle. Getting it inside would be another obstacle, one I was determined to see through.

"You're almost there," Beck coaxed.

Brooklyn snorted next to him, and from the corner of my eye, I caught my best friend jabbing her in the ribs with an elbow.

I blocked out the two of them and shoved the smoke and darkness into the bottle. My eyes met Torent's. Mrs. Augustine was there, slamming a metal stopper onto the bottle, which she promptly spelled, trapping the shadow inside.

All five of us stared at the swirling mist as it clawed and curled around the glass.

"I'll turn it over to the Court. They'll want to keep it secure until it can be destroyed," Mrs. Augustine said, breaking the stunned silence that had followed.

It was done. I was safe. The curse was gone. I loosed a breath of steam that swirled in the cool air as my shoulders slumped in exhaustion. "What was that?"

The wind whipped at Mrs. Augustine's long hair, but her expression remained fixed on the glass bottle. "Darkness ascended," she declared, her gaze lifting to mine. "The blood hex is gone, Mallory. It stops with you."

My throat was too tight to respond. I only nodded, falling into Torent's waiting arms.

# CHAPTER 17

*I* frowned, staring at the scar just under Torent's eye. It had been a week since the Cold Moon Ball—since I rid myself of the blood hex. The jagged cut Torent had received from the smoke of darkness was mostly healed, leaving behind a pink mark over his golden skin. Every time I looked at it, I was consumed with guilt.

His pretty face was marred because of me.

He gave me a lopsided grin, noticing where my attention had wandered. "Chicks dig scars, you know."

To be frank, he really didn't seem to mind the permanent reminder of what went down that night.

We were on Main Street in front of Shelf Indulgence bookstore on our way to Coffee Haven.

"Is that so?" I smiled back, looping my arms around his neck, and lifted up on my toes to softly press a kiss to the mark. "I think you might be right."

His fingers laced around my waist, keeping me snug against his body and moving us to the side of the path. "Are you ever going to tell me?"

I tilted my head to the side, gazing into his sparkling violet eyes.

"Tell you what?" I asked, batting my eyes.

That glimmer in his eyes grew wicked. "That you're madly and deeply in love with me."

My heart began to beat wildly in my chest, and I shook my head. "God, you really don't lack confidence, do you?"

"I want to hear you say it," he murmured, his voice dropping as he leaned in.

How could I possibly resist? Why shouldn't I tell him how I felt? If there was one thing being cursed taught me, it was that life was too short. I needed to live each moment as if it were my last. Torent became the light at the end of the tunnel—a demon. How ironic.

I had planned on telling him how I felt and had been waiting for the right moment. Now was as good as any, although I should have made him suffer for being so arrogant. My fingers played with the hair at the nape of his neck, my gaze locked on his.

"I love you, Torent Stark. Demon and all. Are you happy now?"

"Almost." He took my mouth, fast and hard, trapping me with the hardness of his body. The kiss stole the air from my lungs. "It just so happens that I'm in love with you. You're stuck with me. I'll never love anyone the way I love you, crash car. You're magnetic."

A laugh fluttered up from my heart. "Cute."

Above our heads, pink, blue, and teal lights danced in the skies. Love like I never felt bloomed inside of me. Not an ounce of darkness.

Thank you so much for reading! I hope you enjoyed Torent and Mallory's journey. I'm grateful and honored you chose to read their story.

xoxo

Jennifer

We hope you enjoyed this story in the Havenwood Falls High series of novellas featuring a variety of supernatural creatures. The series is a collaborative effort by multiple authors.

Other books you might enjoy in the Young Adult Havenwood Falls High series:

*Reawakened* by Morgan Wylie
*The Fall* by Kristen Yard
*Awaken the Soul* by Michele G. Miller
*Fata Morgana* by E.J. Fechenda
*Reclamation* by AnnaLisa Grant

Stay up to date at www.HavenwoodFalls.com

# ABOUT THE AUTHOR

J.L. Weil is a *USA Today* bestselling author of teen and new adult paranormal romance, fantasy, and urban fantasy books about spunky, smart-mouthed girls who always wind up in dire situations. For every sassy girl, there is an equally mouthwatering, overprotective guy. She lives in Illinois with her family who puts up with her *Supernatural* and *Harry Potter* fanatics. It's a problem.

You can visit her online at: www.jlweil.com or come hang out with her at J.L. Weil's Dark Divas on Facebook.

# ACKNOWLEDGMENTS

This book would not exist without Kristie Cook. Thank you so much for inviting and letting me be a part of this wonderful and magical world. I enjoyed the challenge!

To the Havenwood Falls team and authors, it has been an absolute joy to take this journey with all of you.

To the readers who continue to show my books so much love, words can't express my gratitude. You continue to uplift me and support me in ways I never thought possible. I am truly lucky.

And to my family, thank you for putting up with all my "just one more sentence" promises, and reminding me to step away from the laptop and enjoy life.

# AN EXCERPT

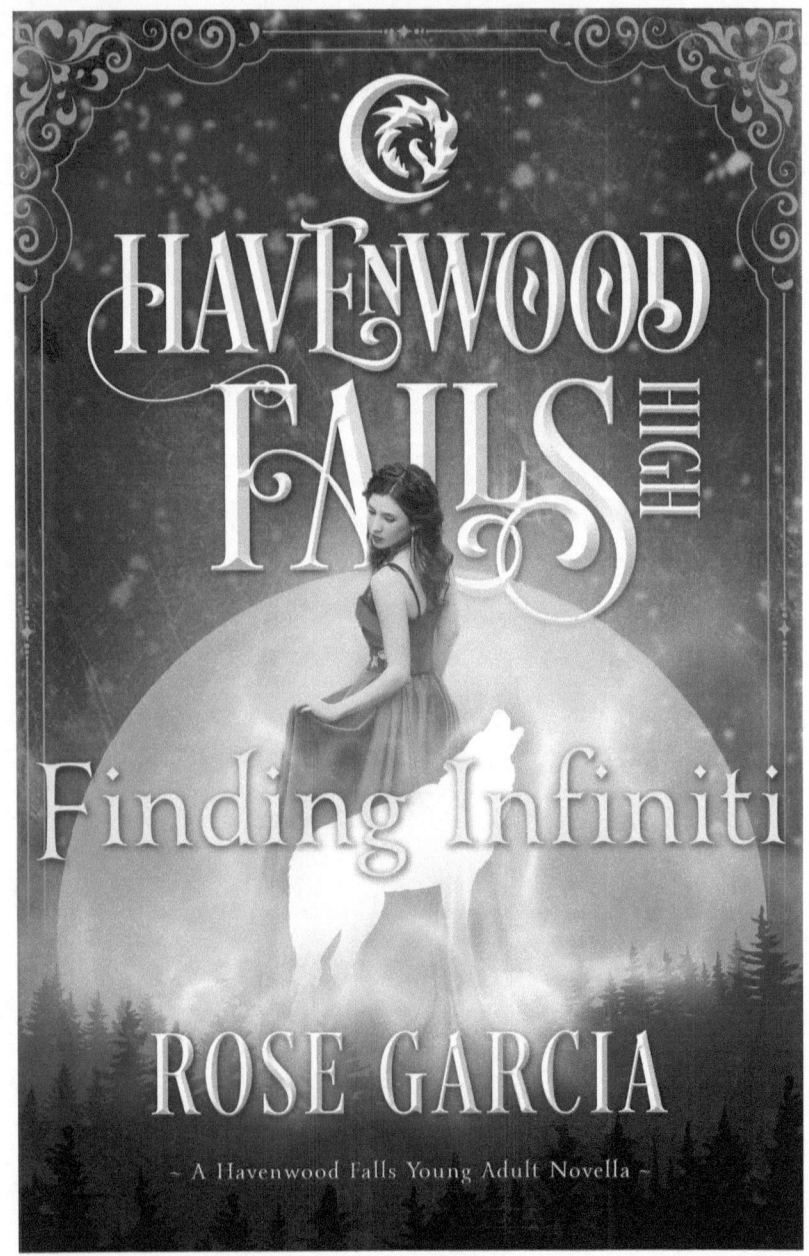

HAVENWOOD FALLS HIGH

Finding Infiniti

ROSE GARCIA

~ A Havenwood Falls Young Adult Novella ~

### *Finding Infiniti* (A Havenwood Falls High Novella) by Rose Garcia

**The highly anticipated sequel to *Saving Infiniti*—can Joe find Infiniti again or is she lost to him forever?**

Joe Greg has reunited with his soul mate Infiniti Clausman only to lose her in a cruel twist of fate. Separated by time and space—and a memory ward that has wiped him from her mind—he vows to do whatever he can to find her, but so far nothing has worked. Believing he'll never be able to see her again, he starts losing all sense of himself. Worse than that, he can't shake the growing feeling that Infiniti's life is in danger . . . again.

Infiniti Clausman is trying to make the most of summer, but something isn't quite right. She feels like she's stuck, as if she can't move on, as if she's missing something or someone. She dismisses the sensation, calling it a case of the graduation blues, but when her psychic neighbor tells her about a quantum event that's been happening since the Cold Moon last December, Infiniti can't ignore the feelings any longer.

Soul mates separated. Memories forgotten. Time slipping. Joe must find Infiniti before it's too late—or he might lose her again, this time for good.

# FINDING INFINITI

## BY ROSE GARCIA

Joe Greg studied every detail of Infiniti Clausman, desperate to sear her image in his brain because he didn't know if he'd be able to find her once she left Havenwood Falls. Long dark hair, ivory skin, the most gorgeous face he'd ever seen. She had time traveled with a Transhuman guy named Fleet from Houston to Havenwood Falls so she could find a protection spell. With their mission complete, they were about to return to their proper place and time, and Joe could hardly bear it. Her magnetic beauty had sparked a connection deep within him, so deep that he was called to her and would be bound to her forever—a wolf shifter and a human. Together against all odds, yet about to be separated in a cruel twist of fate. He knew he'd never be the same without her.

Her lips parted, as if she wanted to say something, just before she vanished from view.

"Infiniti!"

Joe dashed to the spot where she had been standing. Dust particles from Fleet's supernatural energy stream floated in the air. A warm electrical charge filled the cool space. Joe glanced around, as if they'd reappear, but they didn't.

They were gone. She was gone.

Heartbreaking silence filled the room.

"I'm very sorry, Joe," Ms. Howe said in a low voice, still clutching the book she had used to cast her protection spell on Infiniti.

Joe nodded, his heart crumbling. A lump the size of a football lodged in his throat. He felt as if a piece of him had been ripped away. And he didn't know if he'd ever get it back.

"I'll let you have a minute," Ms. Howe added, leaving the room.

Joe couldn't remember the last time he had cried, but watching Infiniti disappear brought hot tears to his eyes. He rubbed them away with the back of his hands, forcing himself not to lose it.

Not here anyway.

He tucked his crutch under his arm, his body throbbing with pain from the wild wolf attack at the Mills Mansion during the Cold Moon Ball earlier. He drew in a deep breath, then hobbled out of Ms. Howe's office and to the front of the herbal shop. He needed to get out of there. He kept his gaze down, avoiding eye contact.

"Thanks for everything, Ms. Howe."

"Sure thing, Joe."

He fumbled with the keys in his pocket as he painstakingly made it out of the shop and into his car. He sat there for a minute, letting the frigid air wrap around his body as the smell of the shop's herbs left his lungs, replaced by the scent of his newly washed car.

Twinkling white, red, and green holiday lights were strung up and down the street. Yet their cheerful and festive message fell flat on Joe. Despair had taken him over. Hours earlier, Infiniti was sitting next to him, dressed like a princess for the ball, and now she was gone. He leaned his head back against the headrest, thinking of their amazing kiss and the promise he had made to find her.

Could he really do it?

He started his car and headed home. Driving through the quiet streets of the town, a slew of memories exploded in his brain. A few months after Infiniti had vanished back in December 2012, he had a series of dreams of horrible things happening to her, incidents that all resulted in her death. Another car accident, being swept away by a tornado, drowning in the ocean, even catching on fire. He shuddered as dread worked its way through him.

He thought of that damn reaper, Shade StormIron, and his words: "The doll's soul still wants me. I can feel it. I'll be back in due time."

A blast of icy fear invaded his senses. Had they sent Infiniti back to 2012 only to die?

He slammed on his brakes and screeched to a halt. He made a U-turn in the middle of the road and sped back to the herbal shop. He parked the car, hopped out, and rushed over to Ms. Howe as she emerged from the door.

"It didn't work!"

She huddled into her long dark coat and wrapped her arms around herself. "What do you mean, it didn't work?"

"We sent Infiniti back to 2012, and she's going to die there! I know it!"

Ms. Howe looked away for a second, as if contemplating the possibility.

"Listen, Joe. I don't know if you're right or if you're wrong, but I do know a thing or two about destiny, and I can tell you that destiny cannot be changed. Not ever." She stared up at the night sky. "It's like telling the moon not to be bright. It simply can't be done." She flashed him a look of concerned sympathy. "So whatever will be, will be."

He looked down at the sidewalk, wracking his brain for a response, when an idea came to him.

"Okay, fine, I get that about destiny, I really do. But what if her coming here was another type of destiny? A way for the right destiny to counter the wrong destiny?" He stopped, thinking his words weren't making any sense, but went on anyway. "I mean, we didn't bring her here, yet she showed up needing our help. Maybe she needs our help again."

He hobbled forward, waiting for the red-haired witch to give him some sign of hope that she understood what he was saying and would help him.

She nodded but held a pensive look on her face. "Maybe she does, Joe. Maybe she does. But let's get through the holidays first, okay? We can take up this conversation later."

"Okay," Joe said, trying to calm his excitement. "That sounds great. I'll come by after the new year. Thank you, Ms. Howe."

Joe felt better, but there was no way he could wait until after the holiday break to do something about finding Infiniti. He got back in his car and drove home, his mind searching for his next move. Once home and in his room, he texted Kase, knowing he'd still be up.

**Me: Dude**

**Kase: Sup**

**Me: Need your help**

**Kase: About the girl? Did it work? My dad told me**

Joe wasn't surprised that Sheriff Ric had said something to Kase about what had happened to Infiniti, and he didn't mind. Kase was his best friend. He would've told him everything anyway.

**Me: Yeah, I think. And now she's gone**

**Kase: Sorry**

**Me: It's ok. But I have an idea. Come over tmr. I'll fill you in**

**Kase: Ok**

Joe set his phone down and lay on his bed, exhausted and feeling like crap. But more than anything, he was determined to find Infiniti Clausman. And no one could stop him.

He turned off his bedside lamp and eyed the streaks of moonlight that poured through the blinds of his window. His mind swirled with different ideas of how he could find her when a soft knock sounded on his door.

"Joe, it's Mom. Can I come in?"

"Yeah, sure."

He sat up and switched his lamp back on. The soft light illuminated his blue-and-gray-hued room. His mom sat on the edge of his bed. Her long blond hair was wet from a recent shower.

"I heard you come in and wanted to check on you." She patted his leg and gave him a reassuring smile. "You okay?"

His fight with the wild wolf pack back at the Mills Mansion had left his body cut and bruised, but nothing could compare to the pain crushing his heart. He rubbed his head, masking his emotions, and focused instead on his physical pain.

"I'm fine. Just a little sore."

She gave him the all-knowing mom look. "I wasn't talking about your wounds, son."

"Oh," he murmured, not wanting to go there with his mom. "You mean Infiniti?"

"Yes, I mean Infiniti."

He thought of telling her his fears about Infiniti returning home only to die, but decided against it. She'd never let him try to find her. Neither would his dad. And really, he couldn't blame them. Try to find a time-traveling human girl he was called to? It was a crazy idea. Besides, they didn't even know he'd been called to her.

Joe shrugged. "She came here to do what she needed to do, and she's gone now."

His mom gave a slight nod. She patted his leg one more time and stood up to leave. "I'm very sorry, Joseph."

"Me too."

Alone again, Joe eased himself back into bed. He stared at the ceiling until the night crawled by and transformed to day. And when Kase finally showed up at his house later that morning, he hadn't slept a wink. He also hadn't formulated a plan for how he was going to find Infiniti.

"Dude," Kase said, looking his friend over. "You look like hell."

"You don't even know the half of it."

Joe limped his way down the hall, leading Kase to his room. He locked the door so they wouldn't be disturbed by his little brother, Boris.

Kase kept staring at Joe's bruised face. "My dad told me you were in a fight, but he didn't mention you got your butt kicked."

"I was swarmed. If that Transhuman guy Fleet hadn't shown up when he did, I don't know what would've happened."

Kase shook his head. "I wish I could've been there for you on that back patio instead of inside the Mills Mansion with Elle. I guess

I was so wrapped up with her, I didn't even catch on that you needed help."

"Well, you can still help. That's why I texted you to come over."

Kase sat on the chair at Joe's desk. His leg bounced. He rubbed his hands together, ready for action. "Sure. Whatever you need."

Joe waited a few seconds before he continued.

"I need you to help me get to 2012."

Kase's eyes widened. He eyed Joe for a minute before laughing. "Uh, what?"

"Infiniti is in trouble. I felt it back in 2012 when she disappeared from the medical clinic, and I feel it again now. So I need to go to her. Right away. Before it's too late and something happens to her."

Joe kept a steady gaze on Kase, letting him know he wasn't kidding. The message finally sank in.

"You're serious?"

"Yeah, I am."

Joe moved across the room. He peered out the window and eyed the wintry landscape, wondering if Infiniti was still alive, when an idea came to him.

"I'm so stupid!" he called out. He snatched his laptop from his backpack and opened it on his bed. He ran a search for Infiniti Clausman Houston.

"Good idea!" Kase said, looking over his shoulder. "We can find her and help her from here. Time travel not required."

Joe's search turned up zero results. "Crap," he mumbled. "Nothing."

"Gimme that." Kase turned the laptop toward him. He typed Infiniti Clausman Texas. He clicked the search button. Still no results.

"Boys!" Joe's mom called from the other side of the door. "I've got some snacks if you're interested."

Joe's fingers hovered over the keys as his mind raced. There had to be a way to find Infiniti online. There just had to be. Or maybe there was no information on her because he was too late and she was dead.

His gut clenched tight. A knot formed in his throat.

"Be right there, Mrs. Greg!" Kase answered. He rested his hand on the laptop screen before closing it shut. He eyed his friend. "Joe, dude. She's back where she belongs, six years in the past. You need to let her go."

Joe knew right then and there that he couldn't involve Kase any further in his search. It'd be too dangerous, too risky. Plus, Kase didn't understand what it was like to be called to someone and have them ripped away. He'd have to go it alone. He forced a smile and put his hand on Kase's shoulder.

"You're right," he blew out, faking defeat. "I need to let her go."

"Exactly," Kase said with an encouraging smile. "Now, let's go eat."

Kase and Joe's little brother Boris dove into a mound of fritule pastries as if they hadn't eaten in days. Joe's mom made the donut-like fried Croatian delicacies every holiday. It was her most prized recipe that had been handed down from generation to generation. Joe usually had no problem matching their enthusiasm for food, especially for fritule, but this time he could barely finish a few bites. His stomach had twisted into a permanent knot, and he couldn't get his mind off Infiniti. Plus, exhaustion was beginning to set in after a night of life-altering events and no sleep.

Joe's mom caught on right away. She started clearing the kitchen table.

"Maybe you should rest, Joe. Take a nap or something. You did have quite the eventful evening."

"Yeah," Joe said, his eyelids so heavy he struggled to keep them open. "I could use a nap."

Kase got up and stretched. "Yep, I could use a nap, too. Thank you, Mrs. Greg." He patted Joe on the back. "See you later, dude."

Joe rubbed his throbbing shoulder, wincing a little from the sting of Kase's pat. He wondered when his wolf-shifter healing abilities would kick in as he retreated to his room. He eased himself onto his bed, his bones so sore he could hardly move. But as tired as he was, his mind was too busy to sleep just yet. Instead, he started formulating his plan. Go to Ms. Howe after the holiday and see if she'd help him. If she couldn't or wouldn't, then he'd have to find someone else to help him time travel to Infiniti. Question was, who could do it? And would they? He wasn't sure, but he was determined to find someone.

With a long yawn, he draped a blanket over himself. His body melded into the soft cotton while exhaustion took over and his brain finally shut off.

$\sim$

Early the next morning, Joe was back at it. He scoured the internet for any mention of a death of a Houston teen girl in 2012 but found nothing that matched Infiniti's description. He took that as a good sign and decided to go with the theory that she was still alive.

With his online search pretty much exhausted, he started looking into time travel. He spent days at the Sun and Moon Academy library reading every book on magic and time travel he could find, but couldn't make any of the spells work for him. He thought of talking to Gallad Augustine or even Addie Beaumont to see if they'd help him, but their connections to the Court of the Sun and the Moon would be too risky. The last thing he needed was to cross the leaders of the town. His dad would be furious.

With the holiday break finally over, Joe went to see Ms. Howe at her herbal shop. She ended up giving him a long explanation for why he shouldn't meddle with fate and destiny. When school started, he subtly brought up the topic of time travel with some of his teachers, but nothing they mentioned helped him.

Days turned into weeks. Weeks morphed into months. Joe was beginning to think he'd never find Infiniti. Desperate and fresh out of ideas, he decided to change his tactic. Instead of searching for Infiniti in the past, he'd search for her in the present. He'd go up and down every single street in Houston if he had to. He didn't care if there was a six-year difference between them. Couples had age differences all the time. And in the larger scheme of things, six years was nothing. But what if he found her and she thought he was crazy? Or what if she was married? Or maybe she really was dead. He forced himself not to think of worst case scenarios. He had to keep trying until he found her.

But still, deep down, he couldn't shake the overriding feeling that he wouldn't be able to find her in the present because something horrible had happened to her in the past.

"Hang on, babe," he said as he started a fresh search on his laptop. "I'm coming."

This time he searched for flights to Houston for after graduation. He scribbled the prices on a piece of paper. Factoring in food and thinking he could sleep on park benches, he'd need at least eight hundred dollars. With the graduation money he thought he'd be getting, plus the money he'd be making over the summer, he'd have more than enough. As for his parents, he knew they'd be pissed, but he didn't care. He had to go.

The seasons changed from freezing to mild to sunny, and before Joe knew it, the end of the school year had arrived. Graduation had come and gone. His friends were either making plans to go away for college or stay nearby and attend the new Sun and Moon Academy College of Supernatural Guardians. He had been invited to be a member of the inaugural class of the college, but had turned it down. He needed to focus on finding Infiniti. Nothing else mattered, and his flight to Houston couldn't come fast enough.

Purchase *Finding Infiniti* where books are sold.